D1358199

RENDEZVOUS WITH MURDER

Slowing down, Rudd drew the car off the road into the opening to a field as her murderer must have done. It was wide enough to take a car, deeply rutted, as it had been on that day four years before . . . For a few minutes, he remained quietly at the wheel. The pilgrimage was almost over. But there was only so much room for sentiment and memories. Facts were what mattered . . .

She had been strangled from behind. The position of the marks on her throat had indicated this. And strangled quickly by someone with strong hands. The attack had been unexpected, too. She hadn't anticipated it. There had been no signs of a struggle; no bruising on her face or body to suggest she had fought for her life.

Bantam Books by June Thomson
Ask your bookseller for the books you have missed

CASE CLOSED

JUNE THOMSON

BANTAM BOOKS
TORONTO · NEW YORK · LONDON

All of the characters in this book are
fictitious, and any resemblance to actual
persons, living or dead, is purely coincidental.

*This low-priced Bantam Book
has been completely reset in a type face
designed for easy reading, and was printed
from new plates. It contains the complete
text of the original hard-cover edition.*
NOT ONE WORD HAS BEEN OMITTED.

CASE CLOSED

*A Bantam Book/published by arrangement with
Doubleday & Company, Inc.*
PRINTING HISTORY
*Doubleday edition published February 1977
Detective Book Club edition February 1977
Bantam edition/October 1980*

*Bantam Books are published by Bantam Books, Inc. Its trade-
mark, consisting of the words "Bantam Books" and the por-
trayal of a bantam, is Registered in U.S. Patent and Trademark
Office and in other countries. Marca Registrada. Bantam
Books, Inc., 666 Fifth Avenue, New York, New York 10103.*

PRINTED IN THE UNITED STATES OF AMERICA

0 9 8 7 6 5 4 3 2 1

For Roy and Tom

1

Detective Inspector Rudd waited in the entrance of the police headquarters car-park for a gap in the traffic in order to turn right. It was half-past six on an evening in early March and already dark and raining hard with that heavy, ruthless, slanting rain that falls as if it never intended stopping. There were few pedestrians about. Those who were out in the streets walked quickly; dark, anonymous shapes huddled under umbrellas. Rudd, inside the car, with the heater on and the windscreen wipers ticking contentedly to and fro, watched them with the comfortable sympathy of someone safely inside in the warm and dry.

A gap came at last in the traffic and he eased the car forward. As he did so, he glanced into the rear mirror and gave a smile of satisfaction. Two cars behind him, a small green van had drawn out of the cul-de-sac in which it had been parked and had also joined the stream of traffic.

For the past three days Rudd had been followed. Or, at least, he had been aware of it for only three days, for the man who was tailing him knew what he was doing. He never got too close and he never used the same car twice.

On the first day it had been a Volkswagen; the second, a mini; tonight, the green van; all small, nondescript cars, well used; the sort one sees everywhere in the streets and doesn't normally notice.

So far, Rudd had no idea who the man was or what he looked like. As he was careful to keep well back, tucked in behind the other traffic, Rudd had not seen his face except for a pale blur behind the windscreen. But the Inspector felt he already knew something about his personality; that he was patient, persistent and, whatever reason lay be-

1

hind his surveillance, it must be something he needed very much to tail the Inspector so assiduously for three days.

Rudd had thought about it a great deal ever since he had first noticed he was being followed. Revenge was the most obvious motive. Although he could think of no possible case, it seemed likely that the man was someone he had sent down on a charge, or possibly a relative or close friend, who bore a deep, personal grudge against him in consequence. It was a risk any policeman had to be prepared to take.

During the first two days, he had braced himself for the expected attack, anticipating that it would come when he was at his most vulnerable, alone, in the car-park behind the headquarters. It was not well lit. It was some distance from the main building. He could be badly beaten up before help came.

On the first evening, he had walked quickly to the car, his keys ready in his hand, so that he would not be standing in the open for longer than necessary. But no attack came. On the second evening, he had almost courted it, walking slowly from the front entrance to the car-park so that the man should have plenty of time to see him. But still he made no move. He had remained seated in his car that was parked across the road in the cul-de-sac and, later, had simply followed the Inspector home, as he had done the previous night.

What *did* he want, then, if it wasn't revenge?

As a tailing job, it was almost professionally carried out. Rudd had to admire the man's skill and patience. He himself had taken part frequently in police surveillance and knew only too well the boredom of long hours of waiting in parked cars, watching a suspect's house, following him day after day as a dossier was built up of the places he visited and the people he met.

The similarity struck him as a possible motive. If the man did not want revenge, could he be following Rudd because the Inspector was in the position to supply him with information he needed? An address, perhaps? Or the whereabouts of someone he was looking for?

He had voiced this new theory to Detective Sergeant Boyce that morning. The burly Sergeant was inclined to be dismissive.

"I still think it's you he's after," he said. "I'll lay you ten to one you'll be found sparked out beside your car one of these dark evenings. You ought to have someone with you."

"No, he's left it too long," Rudd replied. "If that was his motive, he'd've knocked me over the head two nights ago and skipped out fast. You've done tailing yourself, Tom, and you know the longer it lasts, the more chance there is of being spotted. If he's prepared to risk that, he's after something else. Like I said, I think I'm supposed to lead him to some one or some place. At any rate, he wants me to supply him with some information I've got and he hasn't. The trouble is, I don't know what that information is myself at the moment."

"A case you're working on" suggested Boyce.

"I've though of that," Rudd replied, "and there's nothing. As you know yourself, it's been routine paper-work for the past few days."

"Well, then, a case you've been involved in?"

"Nothing much there either. Not big enough to keep a man on my tail day after day, anyway. A couple of break-ins. A pub brawl that resulted in a g.b.h. charge."

"There was that murder," Boyce pointed out, with a slightly aggrieved air, as if Rudd were being deliberately awkward in turning down his suggestions.

"Mrs. Freedman, you mean? But that was purely domestic. No-one outside the family was involved. I wish I could get a look at him. If I knew who he was, I might have a better idea why he's been following me."

"Would you like me to stroll past?" Boyce suggested. "If he's still parked in that cul-de-sac, I could have a dekko."

"No," said Rudd. "We've got to be a bit more subtle than that. There's nothing up that street except houses. If you walk past, all you can do is turn at the dead end and walk back again. He's bound to be suspicious. If he's as sharp as I think he is, he'll spot you at once, and I don't want him to know we're on to him. No, what we've got to do is lure him inside somewhere, where we can take a look at him without making it look too contrived."

He paused, thought for a moment and then added:

"It's Thursday night, Tom. How do you fancy a drink out tonight."

Boyce looked at him and grinned.

"What's the plot?" he asked.

"Something quite simple," Rudd replied. "The past two nights I've spent quietly at home. I think I'll change my routine and see if that forces him to show a bit more of his hand. I'll need you, Lawson and a friendly publican. What about Wally Todd at the Six Bells? He's been helpful in the past."

The plan had been discussed and drawn up in detail and, now, driving home, with the man still on his tail, Rudd settled back comfortably in his seat. With any luck, he'd know who the man was, or at least what he looked like, before the evening was out.

On the outskirts of the town, Rudd turned into the road where he lived with his widowed sister. The van didn't immediately follow him. The man was too clever for that. The street was a quiet, suburban side-turning with hardly any traffic passing along it apart from the residents' cars. The man, therefore, dropped out of sight for a time, either waiting in the main road or driving on a little way before turning and circling back.

Tonight Rudd left his car parked in the drive-in to the house, not putting it away in the garage, as he usually did; a sign that he would be taking it out again later that evening, as he hoped the man would realise. Going indoors, he greeted his sister and then went straight upstairs where he kept watch through the window of the darkened front bedroom. Ten minutes later the green van drove past the house and parked discreetly, as it always did, in the parking bay of a block of maisonettes further up the road. It was a good choice of place. The other cars already there made his presence unremarkable. And there he was prepared to wait, for hours if need be, until the lights in the Inspector's house had gone out and the man was convinced that the occupants had gone to bed. Rudd was already aware of this. He had kept watch the night before from the same darkened bedroom and seen the car drive away at 1:30 A.M., where to he had no idea, but it was another fact the Inspector was hoping to establish before the evening was over.

Going downstairs, he made three telephone calls: one to Lawson, the finger-print expert on the local police force; one to Wally Todd, publican of the Six Bells at Bedstow, a village about seven miles away, and the last to Boyce.

"It's on," he told Boyce. "He tailed me home again tonight. A dark green van this time, registration number EVO 364C. Off-side wing a bit bent."

"That's fine," replied Boyce's deep voice. "I'll pick him up easily."

"I don't want him to know he's being followed," Rudd said quickly. "The man's no fool, so keep well back."

"Don't worry, I will," Boyce assured him and added with a chuckle, "You know, I'm looking forward to this evening. A couple of jars in the Six Bells and a quiet tailing job is my idea of a nice little case."

"I've phoned the others, Lawson and Wally Todd," Rudd went on. "They know what to do. I'll arrive at the Six Bells about ten o'clock, not too early. If we do manage to lure him inside and get a look at him, he may get nervous if he's kept hanging around too long. So I'll turn up about half an hour before closing time, for a quick pint. But I want you and Lawson already there before I arrive. If the man doesn't come in . . ."

"I go out to the car-park and try to get a look at him myself," Boyce put in, "and then tail him after he's followed you home."

"Right!" said Rudd. "I think that's all sewn up, as far as we can, at this stage. See you in the Six Bells later."

He rang off and spent the rest of the evening until it was time to leave comfortably and without impatience. Although the case intrigued him, he was prepared to wait without fretting for the hours to pass. A country upbringing and a natural inclination to take life as it came had given him a certain quiet stoicism and an amused detachment, which showed in his face, the pleasant fresh features of a farmer, the sort of man who leans on gates, ruminating slowly. It had been a useful asset in his career in the police force. It tended to disarm people, as Rudd knew, and he exploited it ruthlessly at times.

Dorothy, his sister, had made beef stew with dumplings, followed by apple crumble, that Rudd ate with enjoyment. Afterwards, he settled down to some paper-work, one of the less appealing sides of police duties, as far as he was concerned, but one that had to be done. At half-past nine, he put on his coat in readiness to go out, saying nothing more to his sister as he kissed her quickly on the cheek, except he wouldn't be home too late.

She did not ask where he was going. She never did, un-

derstanding with quiet instinct that he preferred to keep his
professional and private lives totally separate. Rudd himself
sometimes wondered if her life, housekeeper to a bachelor
brother, was happy and felt guilty that, because of the nature of his work, she was so often alone. But he consoled
himself with the thought that she had her faith and the
little social round that the church community involved her
in and, when he had a free evening, which wasn't often, he
tried to remember to take her to the local cinema.

Outside, he took his time backing the car out into the
road, giving the man plenty of warning. As he drove away,
he saw the van's sidelights were switched on and then he
lost sight of him as he turned into the main road. For a
moment, he wondered if his ruse had failed but, further
down the street as he approached the round-about, he saw
the van, a couple of hundred yards behind him, tucked in
behind a Ford Cortina. Rudd smiled to himself. It looked as
if the plan was going to work, after all.

Bedstow was an attractive village, picturesque enough
and near enough to Chelmsford to have become a commuters' haven. Over the years, the cottages and small houses
that made up the village centre had exchanged hands at
overinflated prices as jaded businessmen, with a longing for
what they imagined was the simple life, bought them up.
The original inhabitants, with more sense, moved out to
the well-built Council house estate, tastefully hidden behind the church, thankfully exchanging the low, beamed
rooms and steep, inconvenient stair-cases for more modern
amenities.

It's location was one of the reasons why Rudd had chosen the Six Bells as a rendezvous. Unlike a genuine village
pub, it drew on a wider clientele. The presence of strangers, like Boyce and Lawson and, if his plan succeeded, of
the man who had been following him, would not atttract
attention. Besides, the Inspector knew the landlord well. A
couple of years before he had investigated a fraud case that
involved a man who had moved into the village and Rudd
had used the pub on that occasion to keep watch on the
suspect, taking Wally Todd into his confidence. Rudd
knew him to be reliable and discreet. He liked Todd, too,
and had kept up the acquaintanceship, dropping in from
time to time for a casual, off-duty drink.

As he approached the village, he glanced again in the rear mirror. The van was still there, following at a discreet distance. Flashing his indicator light, Rudd turned right into the car-park of the pub and, switching off the engine and getting out, ducked through the rain to the entrance at the front of the building. The van, he noticed, had gone past, but this did not worry him. Rudd had no doubt that he had driven on but would turn and come back. Pushing open the door, the Inspector went inside.

The Six Bells consisted of one large room, which was another reason why Rudd had chosen it. Observation would be easy. A long counter ran almost the length of it, on the far side opposite the door, and to the right of it was an area furnished like a bar-parlor with low tables and comfortable chairs, while the area to the left had preserved more of the tap-room atmosphere and it was here that the darts players, the genuine locals and those who liked to think they were, usually gathered.

Even though it was raining, the bar was fairly crowded, Rudd was pleased to notice. Too few people made surveillance more obvious. On the other hand, too many presented problems of another sort. Rudd intended getting a good look at the man. He didn't want him to go to cover in a crowd.

As he approached the counter, he noticed Lawson straightaway, seated to the left, reading the *Guardian*, with a gin and tonic on the table in front of him and putting on, Rudd thought, a good imitation of a businessman playing at being a countryman, in a tweed jacket with leather patches on the elbows. Of Boyce there appeared to be no sign, not that Rudd was concerned. He was there somewhere. Despite his height and bulk, the Sergeant had a talent for fading into the background and taking on, like a chameleon, the aura of his surroundings.

"Evening, Mr. Rudd," Wally Todd greeted him as he approached the bar. He was a big, loose, casual man.

"Evening, Wally," Rudd returned. "A pint of the usual."

As he drew the beer and passed it over the counter, Todd gave Rudd a quick, reassuring smile that meant "Don't worry. We'll play our part." His wife, Stella, blond and cheerful, was concerned in the plan, too. Rudd glanced down the counter to where she was standing, chatting to another customer. She knew what she had to do. Rudd had explained it over the telephone earlier in the day and he trusted that she was sensible enough to carry it through.

Taking his pint and turning away, Rudd appeared to absorb himself in watching some men who were playing darts on the far side of the room. It was a good position to take up for he could keep the entrance under observation without appearing to do so. At that moment, he noticed Boyce for the first time, sitting in the corner, involved in a game of dominoes with two genuine local residents, judging by their appearance. A tiny glance passed between them, imperceptible to anyone else, and then Rudd turned his attention to the darts players.

The door opened at this point and two men came in; neither of them, Rudd realised, his man. They were too obviously together and the man he was looking for was a loner. Talking loudly, they made for the bar and Rudd relaxed.

Ten more minutes passed before the door opened again and, this time, Rudd knew it was his quarry. As if casually watching the player about to throw a dart, he glanced across, but his attention was focussed beyond the man to the newcomer who had just entered. In that fleeting second, before Rudd turned his head, as if following the flight of the dart towards the board, he had taken in the man's appearance and, although he had never seen the man before, he could have filled in a dossier about him.

Height—five feet ten inches. Build—slim. Age—late thirties. Clean shaven. Hair colour—dark brown but probably dyed. It had a dense, matted look that wasn't natural. Complexion—pale, with the pallor that suggests an unhealthy indoor life. Possibly prison? Rudd wondered. He had seen the same pallid skin on men who had served terms of imprisonment.

Clothing—good quality, trendy without being flashy, and looking curiously new. A black car-coat with raglan sleeves, charcoal-grey trousers cut with a bit of a flare; patterned shirt in a blue and green paisley design, worn with a dark blue tie. The fact that all the clothes looked new might also indicate a recent prison sentence, although not necessarily so. But a man coming out after several years spent inside might have to replace his clothes.

There was something else about the man that convinced Rudd he was the one he was looking for: nothing factual, this time, just an impression. The newcomer stood in the doorway for a few seconds, taking his time, looking the place over, before moving quietly towards the bar counter. Rudd had already glanced away before the man's eyes rested momentarily on him but it was long enough to give him a good idea of his character. Quiet, discreet, watchful, suspicious; the same type of personality that had tailed him so patiently and persistently for three days.

Rudd lit a citarette, the agreed signal to Wally that the man had entered the bar, but he made no attempt to turn round. If Wally carried out his instructions to the letter, Rudd knew exactly what was going on behind his back. The man would be served whatever drink he ordered in a plain, unpatterned glass that had already been carefully cleaned and polished for the purpose. Wally would handle it as little as possible. The glass had been marked on its base so that it could be easily picked out afterwards. Lawson had already called at the Six Bells earlier that day to finger-print Wally and Stella so there would no confusion over identifying the man's prints and, if nothing went badly wrong, Lawson would be able to pick the glass up at closing time and get the prints up to Scotland Yard the following day for checking with the files, in case the man had a police record.

Rudd glanced from Boyce to Lawson. The signal of the lighted cigarette had not been lost on either of them. Meanwhile, Rudd went on smoking and drinking his beer and watching the darts players, keeping his back to the man. It was only when the cigarette was finished and he turned to crush it out on the ashtray on the counter that he saw the man, seated at one of the low tables at the far side of the room, a short drink on the table in front of him, whisky possibly. He was not looking in Rudd's direction.

Rudd was again struck by the man's patient, unhurried air and realised that it, too, might suggest he had served a prison sentence. He had seen it himself before in other ex-prisoners of a certain type. Used to wasting time, sometimes years, they acquire this odd quality of dogged repose; a kind of resigned and fatalistic attitude to life passing them by.

"Last orders, please!" Wally was shouting.

On cue, Stella moved out from behind the counter to fulfill her part in the plan, ostensibly collecting up the dirty glasses in readiness for closing time. If, like Wally, she carried out the Inspector's instructions, she would leave the man's glass on the table but clear away the others, in order to make it easier for Lawson to pick it out afterwards.

Rudd finished the last of his beer and, putting the empty glass down on the counter, nodded a farewell to Wally; buttoning his coat, he made for the door. Neither Boyce nor Lawson so much as glanced up as he left. They, too, knew their parts. Boyce's instructions were to follow the man out when he left; Lawson's to shut himself in the gents' lavatory until the pub had closed for the night, then pick up the marked glass and leave. It seemed foolproof. All Rudd could do was hope nothing went wrong.

Getting into his car, he turned out of the Six Bells carpark and headed for home. His active part in the operation was not over. He simply had to wait until a reasonable hour, turn off the lights and go to bed. Boyce would pick it up from there.

Before turning into his road, he checked again in his rear mirror, although he already knew the man would be following behind him, still keeping at that discreet distance. The van was there, as he had guessed. Reaching home, he put the car away in the garage and let himself into the house. His sister, already in her dressing-gown, was sitting quietly by the fire reading. They had a last cup of tea together before she went up to bed, but Rudd waited a little longer. To turn the lights off too early might appear suspicious. The man had, after all, kept watch on the house for two nights. He must already know something of the Inspector's habit of not going to bed until after midnight. On the other hand, Rudd didn't want to keep Boyce hanging about waiting for longer than was necessary. He would be in position just round the corner in the main road, parked in a lay-by, ready to pick up and tail the man as soon as he gave up his vigil on Rudd's house.

At ten to twelve, Rudd switched the telephone bell from the receiver in the hall to the extension by his bed-side. Boyce would phone in as soon as he had tailed the man to whatever address he was staying.

Undressing, he turned off the lights and then went to the

window in the dark to look up the road. The van was in position outside the maisonettes. Satisfied that everything was as usual, he got into bed where he waited for half an hour, lying in the dark, until he heard a car's engine start up. Slipping out of bed and looking again out of the window, he was just in time to see the van drive past the house in the direction of the main road. He climbed back into bed and waited for Boyce's call.

It came at just after 1:30 A.M. Rudd, who had been sitting up in bed reading with the bed-side lamp on, now that there was no need for the house to be in total darkness, picked up the receiver as soon as the telephone rang. Boyce sounded tired but pleased with himself.

"I followed him back," he told Rudd, "to a small garage on the Westfield road. It's a place that deals mainly in minor repairs and has a few used cars for sale on the forecourt; cheap stuff mostly, nothing much above a couple of hundred quid."

That added up, thought Rudd. It explained how the man had been able to get hold of three different cars on the days he had been tailing him. They were either vehicles that the garage had for sale second-hand or possibly customers' cars, in the garage for repairs, that he'd borrowed for the occasion, without necessarily having the owners' permission.

"The interesting thing is," Boyce went on, "the garage is owned by a father and son, name of Beeson. Does that ring a bell?"

"Yes," said Rudd. "It does."

It was more than two years since the Beesons had first come to his notice. They had been suspected of supplying the get-away car in the hold-up of a lorry in the area but, much to his disgust, Rudd had not been able to turn up sufficient evidence against them, although old man Beeson had later been charged with receiving a van-load of tyres, knowing them to have been stolen, and received a twelve-month sentence.

Rudd knew the garage well for he had been in charge when it had been searched. It was a shabby, run-down place, littered with bits and pieces of old vehicles. To one side of it was a house, as neglected as the garage. He remembered the Beesons, too, both out of the same mould: surly, bad-tempered, uncooperative.

"Well," Boyce was saying, "the man I followed is ob-

viously staying there. He parked the van on the fore-court
and went inside the house. Shortly afterwards I saw a light
go on upstairs. I cruised up and down for a time and about
half an hour afterwards the light went out. I hung about
for a further twenty minutes or so and, as nothing seemed
to be happening, I went home."

"Did he know he was being followed?" Rudd asked.

"I don't think so," Boyce replied. "I didn't get too close
and, luckily, there was a lorry between him and me most
of the time. I kept well in behind it, so I don't think he
could have spotted me. Besides, when I drove past the garage, he was just getting out of the van and he didn't even
look round, so it didn't seem he'd suspected anything."

"Good," said Rudd. "Thanks, Tom. Well, with any luck,
if Lawson turns up anything at the Yard tomorrow, we
may know who he is."

He rang off and settled back against the pillows to consider what Boyce had told him. On first reflection it
seemed odd to the Inspector that the man, well-dressed and
sharp-witted, should have got involved with small-time,
squalid crooks like the Beesons but, on thinking it over, he
could see a possible connection. If his assumption from the
man's pallor that he had been in prison was correct, then it
was possible he had got to know Beeson senior either personally, while they were both in prison, or through the net-
work of criminal connections that spreads nation-wide. If
the man needed to know someone in the district who
would keep him supplied with cars and offer him a hide-
out, he need only to ask among his own criminal associates
for the name Beeson to be suggested to him sooner or
later.

Two things, however, were quite clear to Rudd. The
man who was tailing him was no local villain. Rudd knew
them all, or at least the ones who mattered, if not through
personal involvement, then through the information and
photographs that circulated on files through headquarters.
And he was certain he'd never set eyes on him before.

The second obvious fact was that the man was after
something big, something the Inspector could supply; some
information, as he'd said to Boyce, that would lead him to
some person or some place. Otherwise the man wouldn't
spend all this time tailing him.

What it was, he had no idea, and further speculation seemed pointless. He'd just have to wait until he had further information on the man.

All the same, it was intriguing and, although he turned off the light and tried to settle down, it was some time before sleep came.

2

The man was back again the following morning in another mini, blue this time, with a different registration number. Rudd saw it parked in the bay outside the maisonettes as he got his own car out of the garage. The man, Rudd reckoned, must have resumed his vigil early in the morning, before it was likely that the Inspector would leave for work.

He can't be getting much sleep, Rudd thought to himself with some satisfaction as he drove off.

The traffic was heavy on the main road into town, a continuous line of commuters' cars, like Rudd's, heading for the day's work. Now that he was certain the man was behind him, Rudd didn't bother to check again in the driving mirror. He knew what the man would do. It had become almost a routine. Rudd would park his car behind headquarters and go inside the building while the man would circle the block, returning to take up his position in the cul-de-sac, where there was unrestricted parking and where he could keep watch on both the car-park and the front entrance.

"He's back again," he announced to Boyce, who entered the office shortly after he did. "Blue mini, this time."

The Sergeant was all for doing something active.

"We could pull the Beesons in," he told Rudd. "They must know something about him. Come to that, we could have the man in himself for questioning."

"No," said Rudd. "We wait."

He went to look out of the window. It had stopped raining but the air was still full of moisture; a grey day that smeared everything, roof-tops, pavements, even the furni-

14

ture in the room, with a film of damp. He thought of the man sitting out there, behind the wheel of the car. Now that he could put a face to him, he seemed much more real to the Inspector.

"A cat and mouse game," Rudd remarked softly. The point was, which of them was the cat and which the mouse? At this stage, the roles seemed reversible.

Boyce shrugged heavy shoulders. Lacking Rudd's capacity for patience, it seemed to him better to get things moving. Waiting about was simply a waste of time.

"It'd get on my nerves," he admitted, "being followed everywhere I went."

"Lawson will phone in sometime today," Rudd replied, partly to mollify Boyce. "We may be able to make a move then."

It was mid-morning when Lawson rang, trying to sound calm and official but with an undertone of excitement in his voice that told the Inspector he had found out something worthwhile.

"Yes," he said. "You were right in thinking he might have a police record. The finger-prints checked although the photograph looked a bit different. He was fairer in it and wore a moustache. But it's the same man all right. I'll get copies made of both the prints and the photographs to bring back."

So he had dyed his hair, thought Rudd.

Lawson continued, obviously reading from some notes in front of him, "Name, Raymond Arthur Stoll. Age, 37. Address, Seventeen Winchester Terrace, South Kensington. Sent down for two years on a receiving charge."

Another hunch correct. As Rudd had suspected, the man had served a prison sentence.

Lawson resumed his normal voice.

"I managed to have a quick chat with the inspector who handled the case. Stoll dealt mainly in good-class stuff, furs, cases of whisky, consignments of watches, that sort of thing. The Yard suspected he set the thefts up himself, found a customer first and then got the stuff knocked off afterwards by small gangs. But there wasn't enough evidence to make that charge stick. The point was, as soon as the stuff got nicked, it disappeared very quickly afterwards; obviously distributed within hours, before the police had time to find out where it was being stored. Anyway, as I said, they pinned him down at last on the one receiving charge and he got two years in Parkgate. He came out about two months ago."

"Two months?" asked Rudd. "Are you sure?"

That part didn't add up. If the man had been released from prison two months before, why had he waited until now to start tailing Rudd?

"Quite sure," Lawson was saying. "He was released early in January. I haven't got the exact date but I could check if you want me to."

"No, don't bother," Rudd replied. "We've got enough on him to be getting on with for the moment."

"I'll make my way back then," Lawson said and rang off.

Rudd repeated the information for Boyce's benefit.

"Well, we know who he is now," the Sergeant said, looking pleased, as if the whole matter were finally settled.

"Agreed," replied the Inspector. "But it still leaves a good many questions unanswered. Why should a London crook want to tail me so persistently? We still haven't got a solution to that one. And Lawson's information raised another question. If Stoll was released from Parkgate in January, why did he wait until March before he started following me about?"

Boyce pulled a dubious face.

"I still say haul the Beesons in for questioning."

"No," said Rudd with conviction. "That would be really showing our hand. I don't think Stoll knows I've rumbled him. If we question the Beesons he'll realise I'm on to him. Besides, what could the Beesons tell us about Stoll? I doubt if it would be very much. They're small, local fry. Stoll's a receiver on quite a big scale, from what Lawson found out about him, and a sharp operator. I think he's using that garage simply as a base and as a source of supply for cars. It's likely he pays the Beesons enough to make it worth their while but I doubt if either of them know much more about him than that. If we pull Stoll in, he's not likely to tell us much either. Certainly not why he's been following me around for the past three days. What would your answer be, if you were in his shoes, Tom? I know what I'd say. 'Following you, Inspector? Whatever gave you that idea?' Or, alternatively, 'I'm so sorry, Inspector. I thought you were someone else. You look just like a man I know who owes me money.' "

Boyce gave a sudden and unexpected loud laugh.

"You haven't been having it off, have you, with Stoll's wife or girl-friend without realising it?"

Rudd gave him a look and the Sergeant's laughter subsided. Then the Inspector turned back to his contemplation of the view outside the window.

"Something big," he said, half to himself. "And the trouble is I haven't an idea in hell what it can be."

Behind him Boyce said in a subdued voice, "So we go on waiting?"

"Yes, we go on waiting," Rudd replied, "for the cat to jump. Or maybe the mouse."

It was a quarter-past twelve when the telephone rang again. Boyce answered it this time and then passed the receiver over to the Inspector, saying, "It's for you."

"Hello?" said Rudd.

"Detective Inspector Rudd?" a voice asked at the other end. It was a Cockney-genteel voice and oddly familiar, although for the moment the Inspector couldn't think where he had heard it before.

"Yes. Speaking," he replied.

"It's Mr. Tucker here," the voice continued. It was then Rudd realised who the man was. Of course! Donald Tucker, known familiarly as Bibby, a corruption of the popular phrase "best bib and tucker," a nick-name derived years before from Bibby's habit, when he had been a fairly successful pick-pocket, of dressing himself smartly in order to mingle with the fashionable crowds at race-meetings. Bibby had gone down in the world since those palmy days. As he got older and lost his old skill as a dip, he had turned con-man and petty thief.

He had come to Rudd's notice eight or nine years before at a big local agricultural show where he had been passing himself off as a relief waiter in the refreshment marquee and quietly pocketing the takings. He had got, as far as Rudd could remember, twelve months. Since then Rudd had neither seen nor heard anything of the man.

"You remember me, Inspector?" Tucker was asking after a small, embarrassed pause.

"Yes, indeed," Rudd replied blandly. "What can I do for you, Mr. Tucker?"

"It's more a question of what I might be able to do for you," Tucker replied. There was a hesitancy in his voice, as if the man were choosing his words with care, that struck Rudd as odd. From what he remembered of Tucker, he had been a glib talker, never at a loss for something to say.

"A bit of info's come my way that might be useful to you," Tucker went on.

"Really?" said Rudd. He winked at Boyce. "That's extremely kind of you, Mr. Tucker."

The irony seemed lost on the man.

"Anything to oblige," he said, as if eager to help.

"Would you care to come round to the office?" Rudd asked.

Again there was a small pause before Tucker replied, "I'd rather not, if it's all the same to you. Perhaps we could meet somewhere in the town." He added a little too quickly, as if anxious to explain, "I just happened to be passing through."

That's a lie for a start, thought Rudd. He's come down here especially. Glancing at his watch, he said, keeping his voice noncommittal, "It's getting on for lunch-time. What about meeting somewhere for a drink?"

"I don't drink, Inspector," Tucker said primly.

Rudd remembered then that this was true. Tucker was a teetotaller and a non-smoker, unusual qualities among criminals, and, Rudd remembered, too, that Tucker had been proud of his abstinence, as if, in some curious way, it off-set and excused his other short-comings.

"What about a cafe, then?" Rudd suggested, thinking quickly. "There's one in Tower Road, just behind the Odeon. It's called the Blue Boy. It's quite a clean, respectable sort of place."

It had other more practical advantages, which was why the Inspector had chosen it. Parking would be no problem. Rudd would arrive by car and so presumably would Stoll, who would tail the Inspector there. It struck him then that Tucker's telephone call had come a little too pat, as if on cue. Could it be connected with Stoll? It seemed unlikely. Anyway, for the moment, there was not time to think the question out to any depth. Tucker was saying:

"I expect I'll find it."

"I'll meet you there in half an hour," Rudd replied.

Ringing off, he turned to Boyce, who was exuding curiosity, and said quickly, "I'll explain later, Tom. I want a man sent round to the Blue Boy cafe straightaway. Lawson's still not back from London so it had better be Kyle. I'm meeting Tucker there in half an hour and I want Kyle planted before Tucker arrives. He's to tail Tucker. I want tabs kept on him."

When Boyce left the office to put this into operation, Rudd gave his mind over to the question of a possible connection between Stoll and Tucker. It still didn't seem likely. Even in his hey-day, Tucker had never been a big-time crook and when Rudd had met him, he was already past his prime and that was eight years or more ago. Rudd did a rapid mental calculation. Tucker must be all of fifty-five now, if not older. Besides he had never been, as far as Rudd knew, London-based. He preferred moving about the country, from town to town, wherever there was a large public gathering, like a race-meeting or a county fair; lifting wallets and hand-bags and, when he got too old for that, passing dud cheques or conning the more gullible into parting with cash for non-existent services, such as cut-price insurance or a second-hand car going cheap. As a criminal the only advantages he possessed were a plausible manner, a certain native quickness of wit and, when he was younger, an attractive, ingenuous charm that, combined with his good looks and the care he took over his appearance, disarmed his victims into thinking he was a thoroughly nice man to know.

On the other hand, Stoll was a London crook, a receiver, a man who, if the Yard's suspicions were correct, organised theft on a fairly large scale. He certainly worked as fence for the gangs who stole the property.

Given these facts, what possible interest could Stoll have in Tucker? Stolen property was not in Bibby's line of crime. He went for the quick cash return. Besides, he was a loner. Even when he was a dip, he never worked with an accomplice as some pick-pockets do. In addition to that, Tucker was a relatively small fish in the criminal pond.

But then, the Beesons were even smaller fry and Stoll had evidently found them useful.

Was that the possible answer? That Rudd was to lead

Stoll to Tucker because Tucker would be useful to him? Of all the solutions that presented themselves, this seemed the most likely. And yet Rudd could not shake off the feeling that it involved something big and Bibby Tucker couldn't be considered big in anybody's reckoning.

He was still mulling it over when Boyce came back into the office. "Kyle's on his way," he announced and added inquisitively, "Tucker?"

"Bibby Tucker," said Rudd. "Remember him?"

"Can I forget him?" Boyce replied happily. "His face when we picked him up in that refreshment tent, with his little white waiter's napkin over his arm and his back pocket stuffed with money! But that's years ago. Why's he turned up here after all this time?"

"According to Tucker, he's got some information that might be of use to me," Rudd replied and went on to explain briefly his theory that Tucker was in some way tied in with Stoll. Boyce looked unconvinced.

"It could just be a coincidence Tucker phoning up this morning," he pointed out.

"Could be," Rudd agreed. "But Stoll's been tailing me for three days now, as if waiting for something to happen. Nothing much has happened, except for routine office work, until today. Then our old friend Bibby telephones out of the past, 'just happened to be passing through,' as he took such pains to point out."

"Tucker's not a happening," Boyce objected. "He's a non-event."

"Well, we'll see," said Rudd.

A phrase he had used earlier in the morning returned to his mind. A cat and mouse game. It suddenly struck him that, if the simile were applied to Stoll and Tucker, then Tucker would certainly fit the role of the mouse. And the point of the game was, the mouse usually finished up dead.

He voiced his thoughts out loud.

"Tom," he said, "you remember we talked over possible motives and agreed that revenge seemed a likely one? We know now that it's not me that Stoll is after but it could be Tucker. If Stoll has a grudge against Bibby, then I could be set up to lead Stoll to him. Tucker may be a non-event but I'd hate him to finish up literally as a dead loss and feel I'd got his blood on my head."

He stopped there and added quickly, "No, that doesn't make sense. There's no possible way that Stoll could have known Tucker was going to phone me this morning to arrange a meeting, unless Tucker told him himself, and, if Stoll's after Tucker's blood that doesn't seem very likely."

"I get your drift," said Boyce. "But even if Stoll is after Tucker, the Blue Boy cafe is hardly a likely setting for a gang revenge. I can hardly imagine Stoll gunning Tucker down among the tea-urns and the cheese sandwiches."

Rudd laughed. "You're right. My trouble is I've gone over this case so often in my mind, not only can't I see the wood for the trees, I'm beginning to lose sight of the trees as well. All the same, Tom, I'd like you there. Not inside the cafe. Tucker knows you by sight and I don't want to frighten him off by two of us turning up. But if I'm right and Stoll follows me to this meeting, then I'd be happier if you were around, if only to keep an eye on Stoll. You'd better put on some sort of disguise in case Bibby spots you. Could you come in a plain brown wrapper or a beard or something?"

"I'll wear my pork-pie hat and my small ginger moustache," Boyce said promptly. "My old woman once passed me in the street without recognising me, so if they fooled her, they ought to fool Tucker."

"Fair enough," replied Rudd. "Before we go, let's quickly run over the plan. I'll go out by the front entrance and pick up the car. Stoll will presumably follow me. Meanwhile, you slip out by the back of the building and follow Stoll."

"We're going to be quite a little procession, aren't we?" remarked Boyce.

Rudd glanced at his watch.

"I told Bibby I'd meet him in half an hour. It's nearly that now, so we'd better push off straightaway. Kyle ought to be in position inside the cafe. Don't forget Stoll's driving a blue mini today. I've given you the registration number?"

"Don't worry," said Boyce. "I'll be behind him."

Rudd put on his coat, and, going down the stairs, left the building by the front entrance, as arranged. As he started the car, he saw Boyce coming out by the back door, which led directly into the car-park, looking surprisingly different with the addition of the pork-pie hat and moustache, like a

not too successful door-to-door salesman, Rudd thought
with amusement. He waited until the Sergeant had got into
his own car and then drove slowly forward, turning left out
of the car-park entrance.

The blue mini came into view halfway down the High
Street. Of Boyce's car there was no sign. Presumably he
was further back, still in the line of traffic.

Rudd took his time, keeping his speed down to below
thirty. He didn't want to risk Stoll losing him. Or Boyce
losing Stoll. As Boyce had said, they were quite a little
procession.

As he turned into the side-street where the Blue Boy
cafe was situated, he checked that the mini was still behind
him. But, as he drew into the kerb to park, it passed him
and went on towards the end of the road. Not that it worried Rudd. As had happened the previous evening at the
Six Bells, Stoll would turn somewhere and come back.

Taking his time, Rudd got out of the car, locked the
door and sauntered across the road to the cafe. A quick
glance up the street showed Boyce's car coming into sight
round the corner and drawing in at the road-side, several
car-lengths away from where Rudd was already parked.

Once again the plan seemed to be working smoothly;
only unlike the operation at the Six Bells, there was the
additional character of Bibby Tucker to be taken into consideration, with whom Rudd was about to take a friendly
cup of tea.

It's a bit like the Mad Hatter's tea party in *Alice*, Rudd
thought with a grin, and if he extended his earlier simile
into the Lewis Carroll world of seemingly inconsequential
events, then Bibby would have to be the dormouse who
finishes up in the tea-pot.

Rudd suddenly remembered a detail of the last time he
had seen Tucker. It was after he had been arrested and
Rudd was interviewing him in one of those bleak, imper-
sonal rooms, furnished only with the regulation table and
two chairs, that police headquarters provide for such occasions.

Bibby, still in his white waiter's jacket, had sat on one
side of the table while Boyce laboriously counted out the
money they had found on him: thirty-nine pounds in loose
notes, together with another twelve in a woman's purse
that had been secreted in an inside pocket.

Bibby had accepted his arrest philosophically. It was, after all an experience he had gone through many times before. But he had refused, with a shrill and tenacious persistence, to say anything until someone brought him a cup of tea.

"I've been rushed off my feet all day," he protested with an aggrieved air.

Rudd remembered the disgusted look on Boyce's face when Rudd had sent him to the canteen to get Bibby one.

Still smiling at the memory of it, Rudd pushed open the door of the Blue Boy cafe and went inside.

3

The cafe had not many customers in it, for the small local factory and work-shops for which it largely catered had not yet knocked off for the one o'clock dinner hour. A few people sat at the plastic-topped tables, including Kyle, who had evidently decided to make the most of the assignment and was eating his way steadily and placidly through a plateful of fried plaice and chips. He was ideal for a tailing job, being so ordinary and nondescript in appearance that even Rudd had difficulty at times in remembering what he looked like. Bibby Tucker had not yet arrived.

Rudd took a tray and moved along the self-service counter. He'd have to buy something to eat, but the choice main dishes, fish or steak pie with chips and bright green peas, did not appeal to him. He chose cheese sandwiches instead and a cup of coffee, paid and carried the tray over to a table for two against the far wall, laying his overcoat over the other chair to keep it vacant for Bibby when he arrived.

While he ate his sandwiches, Rudd looked round the cafe. It was some time since he had been in it and he was pleased to see it hadn't changed. It was the sort of place he liked, homely and unpretentious, that gave good value for money, serving huge helpings of plain food and cups of strong, dark tea to the workmen who mainly frequented it. A Pirelli pin-up-girl calendar was fixed to one wall and behind the cash register was displayed a collection of picture post-cards of last year's summer holidays, sent by the regular customers: exotic views of beaches in Majorca and the Costa del Sol; more homely ones from Margate and Brixham.

From where he was sitting, Rudd had only a restricted view through the window of the street outside. He could just see Boyce's car but not Stoll's, and he had to assume that Stoll had returned and was parked somewhere near.

Tucker arrived shortly afterwards. As he pushed open the door and stepped inside, Rudd took in his appearance with one rapid, appraising glance. He had changed a lot since the Inspector had last seen him. The thick, dark, wavy hair that had been so much a part of his good looks had thinned and was turning grey. The boyish features had sagged, too. He looked old and pathetic. He had clearly come down in the world as well. All the same, he was struggling to keep up appearances. His suit, though shabby, was carefully brushed and pressed and he sported a handkerchief, double-folded into two peaks, in his breast-pocket. But there was an air of desperate, genteel poverty about him now.

Catching sight of Rudd, he smiled, the old smile that Rudd remembered; that was switched on quickly, like a light, and was designed, and no doubt rehearsed, to crinkle up the corners of his eyes in the most charming manner. But even the smile had a used, second-hand look about it.

Rudd nodded back a greeting and Bibby went off to get himself something to eat at the counter. He came back with two slices of plain, buttered toast and a cup of tea. Seeing them, Rudd regretted that he had not offered to buy Bibby's lunch. Was the man so hard-up he could afford nothing more substantial to eat than that?

"Is that all you want?" he asked as Bibby sat down opposite him.

"I'm on a diet," Bibby told him and patted his waist-line. "I have to watch the figure, you know."

Rudd felt a twinge of pity for the man. He might be a menace to society but, at that moment, he was nothing more than a pathetic, shabby little man, with a strong in-stinct for survival and a streak of courage in him that Rudd recognised for the first time and could not help ad-miring. He noticed, too, how pale he was. It was the same pallor he had seen in Stoll but, in Bibby's case, need not necessarily mean a recent term of imprisonment although, knowing his criminal habits, the twelve months' sentence he had received after Rudd arrested him eight years before had probably not been his last. His pallor could have been simply the result of an unhealthy diet: too many cups of tea and slices of toasted bread.

"Well!" said Rudd, looking deliberately cheerful. "How's the world treating you, Mr. Tucker?"

"Not too badly, Insp . . ." Tucker began, and then, looking carefully round the cafe, added, "Mr. Rudd."

So it's to be a friendly, unofficial chat, thought Rudd, noticing the change in the form of address, although Bibby had always pretended a fastidious dislike of mixing with anybody to do with the law, on both sides of it. Part of his façade was that of the upright, honest citizen.

Rudd bit back a ridiculous desire to ask, "Been in any good nicks recently?" in the same tone of voice one might ask, "Read any good books recently?" The conversation had the polite social gloss to it of two respectable people meeting after several years' absence that struck the Inspector as both funny and absurd. Instead he said, lying to please Tucker:

"You haven't changed all that much."

Tucker was clearly flattered by the compliment.

"Haven't I?" he asked. "And I can't say the years have done much to you either, Mr. Rudd."

The Inspector chewed down the last of his cheese sandwich and settled back in his chair. It was time, he decided, that the polite preliminaries were over. Tucker must be brought to the point.

"I believe you said on the phone that you had some information I might find useful," he said bluntly.

Tucker's demeanour changed instantly. The bright, social expression disappeared. He became nervous and ill at ease, running his tongue over his lips.

"That's right, Mr. Rudd," he replied too quickly. "I thought I'd pass it on, for old time's sake. You were good to me, you know. I've always appreciated that."

Rudd said nothing, but looked encouraging.

"Well, I was in this pub," Tucker went on, in a rush of words. "I'd arranged to meet a friend there; I can't remember the name of it but it's somewhere off the Strand."

It was unlikely to be true, Rudd thought. Not only had Tucker refused to meet him in a pub, a fact that he appeared to have forgotten, but years of experience in interviewing people had taught the Inspector to doubt any story that had too much circumstantial detail in it.

"And while I was there, waiting for this friend, I happened to overhear a conversation," Tucker was saying, "between two men. I couldn't see either of them. They were on the other side of the bar, behind a sort of screen and I couldn't catch all they said, but I did hear the name 'Rudd' mentioned and the word 'Essex' and, naturally, it made me prick my ears up."

"Go on," said Rudd.

He noticed that beads of sweat had appeared on Tucker's top lip and it struck him that the man was not only ill at ease but frightened as well. The words "cat and mouse" came back into his mind and he thought of Stoll, sitting out there in his car somewhere in the street. But there was no time to follow up this line of thought for Tucker was plunging on with his story.

"Like I said, I wasn't able to catch all the conversation, but I did manage to pick out a few words here and there."

He paused at this point. Evidently he had reached the important part of what he wanted to say.

"I also heard the name 'Milly' or possibly 'Molly' mentioned, I couldn't tell you exactly which, but I got the impression they were talking about a case you'd been involved in a few years back."

Again, he ran his tongue over his lips.

"I don't know if the name rings a bell with you, Mr. Rudd?" he asked with an odd note of appeal in his voice.

For a few seconds, the name meant nothing to Rudd. Milly or Molly? He couldn't remember being on a case that involved a woman with either of those names. And then something stirred in his memory, although he was careful not to let any outward sign of it appear on his face. Of course! What had fooled him for the moment was the fact that Bibby had got the name wrong. It was Melly, Melanie Thorpe, whose body had been found dumped in the bushes at a road-side more than four years before. The girl's murderer had never been found and the case remained unsolved.

"I'm afraid the name means nothing to me," Rudd lied, sounding puzzled. "Have any idea what case it was? Theft? Fraud?"

Bibby shook his head.

"I'm sorry, Mr. Rudd, I have no idea."

"Or how long ago it happened?" Rudd went on. "I get a

good few inquiries come my way; too many sometimes.
Was this Milly or Molly, whoever she was, a witness?"

But Bibby seemed genuinely not to know.

"That's all I heard. I wish I could tell you more, Mr.
Rudd," he replied.

"And you didn't get a look at either of these men?"

"Sorry, no. They were behind this partition and then the
friend I was waiting for arrived and we got talking and
they must have left by the other door without me seeing
them go."

"What were their voices like?" Rudd persisted. "Would
you recognise them if you heard them again?"

"I only heard the one man talking," Bibby replied, "and,
like I said, I only caught a word here and there of what he
was saying. It seemed an ordinary sort of voice. Nothing
much special about it; but a Londoner I should say. I defi-
nitely wouldn't be able to identify it, if I heard it again."

The last remark was made with such a curious insistence
that it made Rudd wonder if Bibby didn't, in fact, know
the identity of the man. Storing this impression away for
later consideration, he went on with the questioning.

"How long ago did this happen?" he asked.

Bibby looked flustered.

"Did what happen, Mr. Rudd?" he asked. He was
clearly playing for time.

"You overhearing this conversation," Rudd explained,
although the point of the question ought to have been clear
to Bibby. It was obvious to him that he hadn't bothered to
think out this part of the story in detail, a fact that further
convinced Rudd that he was lying.

"I'm not sure," Bibby replied, after a pause in which he
seemed to recover some of his former glibness. "Time flies,
as they say. It could have been a couple of months ago;
could have been longer."

"I see," said Rudd, keeping his voice non-committal.
"And that's all you heard? The word 'Essex,' my name and
this girl's, whoever she is?"

Bibby lowered his eyes and Rudd realised there was
something else that Tucker wasn't sure whether to admit to
or not. The Inspector waited.

"There was one other word," Tucker said. "It doesn't
make sense to me, but I'll pass it on just in case you find it
useful. It was 'transit.'"

"Transit?" repeated Rudd, genuinely puzzled. The word in connection with the Melanie Thorpe case meant nothing to him.

"It sounded like that," Bibby replied. "And that's the lot, Mr. Rudd, I swear."

Rudd sized him up quickly. He was convinced that there might very well be much more than the little Bibby had admitted, but it was clear he was not going to divulge it at this stage, at least.

"I hope I haven't wasted your time," Bibby added.

"Not a bit," Rudd replied blandly. "I must admit I don't know what all this adds up to but any information's better than none. I only wish I could think what case it could be."

He shook his head as if bemused.

"You could look up your records, couldn't you?" Tucker asked a little too eagerly. "You might come across the name."

"Well now," said Rudd slowly, with feigned reluctance, "I could, I suppose. The trouble is, time. There's not a lot of it to spare. But we'll see. If you could give me your address, Mr. Tucker. I might need to get in touch with you, if I should happen to remember the particular inquiry these men were talking about."

Bibby's eyelids flickered, a sign Rudd remembered from the last time he had interviewed him, a sign of a reluctance to give anything away.

"I haven't got a settled address at the moment, Mr. Rudd. My business"—and here he gave a small, embarrassed cough—"takes me about the country quite a bit. But I could give you the phone number of a cafe where I call from time to time. I know the man who runs it and he could probably get a message to me if you needed to see me again."

It was said with the air of a man who is putting himself out to be obliging.

"Fine," said Rudd. "If you'd just jot it down for me."

Producing a small address book from an inside pocket, Bibby tore out an unused page and, scribbling down a telephone number on it, handed the slip of paper to Rudd, who put it away in his own wallet after glancing quickly at it. It had the London code, 01.

Tucker rose to his feet, holding out a hand.

"It's been very pleasant meeting you again, Mr. Rudd," he said.

Rudd shook hands with him with a show of friendliness that wasn't altogether a pretence. Although Tucker was a crook, there had never been anything really vicious in him; just the pathetic and ignoble desire to make a living at somebody else's expense and even at that he hadn't shown any outstanding talent.

"Thank you for your trouble, Mr. Tucker," Rudd said.

He watched Bibby leave the cafe. After a few moments, Kyle rose to his feet also and followed him out. Rudd doubted if Bibby would notice him. While he and the Inspector had been talking, the cafe had filled up. People were coming and going all the time. Stoll, too, would probably not notice him either.

It crossed the Inspector's mind that if Stoll followed Tucker, as Rudd assumed he would, then it would have to be on foot. Although he hadn't seen Bibby arrive, he doubted if it had been by car. The man's general appearance suggested money was short and owning a vehicle would be beyond his present means. Stoll would presumably abandon his car, returning to pick it up sometime later, after he had followed Tucker to wherever he was staying. The old fear that he had voiced to Boyce earlier that morning returned to his mind: that Stoll for some motive of personal revenge was seeking Tucker's life. Boyce's objection, that it was unlikely to happen in the Blue Boy cafe, had made sense at the time. But the circumstances had changed since then. Tucker was now out on the streets, exposed and vulnerable.

It was true Kyle was tailing him and Kyle was good at his job. All Rudd could do was to hope that Kyle's presence would offer Bibby some protection should Stoll attack him, if that was Stoll's intention. And if it were, it would seem unlikely he would attack straightaway. After all, he had followed Rudd about for three days. He would, no doubt, show the same patience and control over Tucker and it might, therefore, be possible to warn Tucker of the danger and move him to a safe, secret address before Stoll attacked.

There was nothing much more he could do about it, anyway, and he turned his attention to the murder of Melanie Thorpe.

Although he would have to read up the reports when he returned to his office in order to refresh his memory of the details of the case, the broad outlines were still very clear. She had been not quite sixteen, a small, thin girl—really, no more than a child—with light brown hair and one of those awkward, bony faces that might, in an older woman, be described as "interesting." Rudd remembered it vividly, turned up blindly to the sky among the nettles and wind-blown litter near a gate opening on a country road. The overnight rain had draggled the light hair and smeared the little make-up she had worn, giving the dead face a grotesque, sad clown's appearance. She had been a hairdresser's apprentice: more at her mother's wish, he imagined, than her own. From inquiries among her few friends he had learned that she herself wanted to work with animals, "Melly really loved them," one of them said.

It seemed doubly pathetic to Rudd at the time that her life had ended so early, choked out of her, before she even had time to make of it what she wanted.

Her killer had never been traced, although inquiries had gone on for almost a year; so the case had, in fact, never been closed. At the time, the only possible explanation seemed to be that she had been murdered, by a motorist who offered her a lift home. Two factors, however, suggested this might be unlikely. In the first place, she had not been sexually assaulted and Rudd could see no other motive except a sexual one for a man to give a lift to a girl on a lonely country road and then to kill her. Secondly, her mother had insisted, and went on insisting, that Melanie was not the type to accept lifts home from strangers. The other people who knew her agreed. She was a quiet girl, a bit on the timid side.

But exhaustive inquiries had turned up no other more likely explanation and it was this one that, unofficially, had been accepted. Some man had stopped his car while she waited at the bus stop, offered her a lift, which she had accepted, and driven her about half a mile up the road where he had parked in a gate opening, strangled her and then dumped her body over the gate where it was found the next morning by the farmer who owned the field. It seemed then, and it still seemed, a curiously motiveless murder.

And now, here was Bibby Tucker, turning up out of the

past with an elaborately circumstantial story about overhearing a conversation between two men in a pub that re-
ferred to that murder of four years ago. Not that Bibby
realised this, Rudd was convinced. But he had certainly
found out something, God alone knew exactly where or
how. Stoll, too, played some part in it, although what it
was Rudd had no idea.

A receiver of stolen goods, a petty thief and a murdered
girl. A strange trio. And yet something must link them together.

Faces. They seemed to come into Rudd's mind separately, like three images flashed one after each other on a
screen. Stoll's, watchful and alert, with that matted, dark
hair; Tucker's with the little beads of sweat breaking out
on his upper lip; Melly's staring upwards.

He suddenly remembered hers too vividly from that
spring morning all those years before: the mouth fallen
open and the thin, glistening thread of silver across her
forehead left by the track of a snail.

The obscenity of the image revolted him and, crushing
out his cigarette in the ash-tray, he got up abruptly and
made for the door.

Coming out into the damp air of that nondescript side-
street was like emerging into a sane world. Shrugging into
his overcoat, he absorbed the glorious normality of it all:
the decent net curtains at the windows of the little houses,
milk-bottles left on door steps, the corner shop with its
placard advertising Wall's ice-cream. Above the slate roofs,
a work-shop chimney trickled lazy, pale grey smoke.

He noticed then Boyce seated in his car a little distance
down the road and, in his relief, he almost raised a hand in
greeting. But before he had time to do so, the Sergeant
moved his head, a small quick gesture that was meant as a
warning.

Rudd glanced to his right. Further up, beyond where his
own car was standing, the blue mini was still waiting. Stoll
hadn't followed Bibby after all.

The shock of seeing him non-plussed the Inspector for a
moment. He hesitated at the kerb-side, covering up his
confusion by pretending to feel in his pocket for the car
keys.

What the hell *was* going on? What game were they playing? He lost the sense of tragedy he had felt in remembering Melly's death in an absurd anger that was directed toward Stoll and Tucker. Both of them were involved, he knew that now, and a lot of his anger was turned towards Bibby. He even regretted his moment of compassion for the shabby little crook. It was a game, the point of which he didn't know. Or the rules. Or the stakes involved.

But one thing he was sure of—he'd bloody well nail Stoll and Tucker and the girl's murderer before the game was over.

It crossed his mind briefly that either Stoll or Tucker might have killed her. No, not Tucker, he decided almost at once. Tucker had come to him with the information he'd overheard. He'd hardly do that if he had killed her. On the other hand, Stoll might very well fulfill the role of murderer. But why should Stoll, a London crook, have wanted to kill a sixteen-year-old hairdresser's apprentice in the first place?

At this point, Rudd gave up. He needed Boyce to talk it over with; he would listen and agree and raise objections. Turning it over and over in his own mind was getting him nowhere. Besides, in his present angry state, rational thinking was impossible. Boyce would calm him down. There was something stolid and imperturbable about Boyce that Rudd needed. Even the Sergeant's lack of imagination was, under these circumstances, an asset. He worked on facts with the dogged persistence of a blood-hound. He might only rarely raise his nose, so to speak, from the ground to perceive the broader landscape of a case and he hadn't much conception of the subtler workings of the human mind. People in Boyce's opinion came under two headings, the good and the bad, that was all. But what he did have that Rudd knew at times he himself did not possess were lack of temperament and the ability not to get emotionally involved. Yes, thought Rudd, I've got to calm down and talk it over with Boyce.

Still inwardly fuming, he stumped across to the car and, unlocking it, got inside and started the engine. Driving on past the mini, he didn't even bother to give Stoll so much as a sideways glance. He'd be there, soon enough, on his tail.

At the traffic lights for the intersection into the High

Street, he almost drove across them on the amber but re-
sisted the childish temptation to get the better of Stoll by
giving him the slip.

Behind him, the blue mini drew up with Boyce at its
rear. Suddenly the absurdity of the situation struck the Inspector and he began to laugh. He was still laughing when
the lights turned green and he moved off, heading back
towards the office.

4

As he turned left at the lights, Rudd lost Boyce, the Sergeant driving straight on into Adelaide Road, a sensible decision on his part, Rudd thought. Stoll would have tumbled to him sooner of later if he had continued to follow them back to headquarters. He guessed what Boyce would do: drive round the town for half an hour or so before returning to the office.

While he waited for him, Rudd made two telephone calls. The first was an internal call to the records department in the building to ask the sergeant on duty to find and bring to his office the file on the Melanie Thorpe case. The second was to the central records office at Scotland Yard, where he requested details on Bibby Tucker. As this would take a little time to look up, he gave his telephone number so that he would be rung back.

Boyce came in shortly afterwards, looking his usual self, without the hat and moustache, congratulating himself on his ruse.

"You noticed I dropped out?" he asked Rudd. "I thought it best. As a matter of fact, I drove back to the Blue Boy and got myself a poached egg on toast. Sitting outside watching you and Kyle stuffing yourselves with food made me realise how hungry I was." He laughed suddenly. "I wonder how Stoll manages for meals? Do you suppose the Beesons do him up a packed lunch?"

Seeing the serious expression on Rudd's face, he added, "It shook me when he didn't follow Tucker. When Bibby left, with Kyle on his tail, I was bloody sure Stoll would fall in behind, too."

"So was I," Rudd admitted. His previous mood of

amusement had gone, also his anger. He just felt tired and baffled. "All right, so it was a hunch that didn't come off, but there's too much about this case that doesn't make sense to me, Tom. Will you bear with me if I talk it through and try bouncing a few theories off you?"

Boyce sat down in one of the chairs that creaked under his weight.

"I'm listening," he said.

"Well, in the first place," Rudd began, "Tucker's information that he was so anxious to pass on to me amounted to this: he overheard, or said he overheard, two men talking in a pub. Now Tucker's a teetotaller and, when he rang me here this morning and I suggested we meet for a drink, he refused. So, point number one, I feel Tucker was lying."

"Lying about the pub, but not necessarily about overhearing a conversation?" Boyce asked.

"Right," said Rudd, "although it's difficult to tell with Tucker when he is telling the truth."

"What were these two men talking about?"

"I'll get on to that in a moment," Rudd replied. "Let me work through it in my own way. Point number two, Tucker said he didn't see either of these two men and, in fact, heard only one man's voice at all clearly, but when I asked him if he'd recognise it again, he insisted he wouldn't. Now, you know Bibby, Tom. You took part when we interviewed him here after his arrest. Do you remember the way he had of flatly denying something in such a positive manner that made you damned sure he was lying?"

"Yes, I do," Boyce said promptly. "He'd look you straight in the eyes and swear black was white."

"Good," said Rudd. "That confirms an impression I had that Tucker knew the identity of the man he overheard but wasn't going to admit it. You follow me?"

"So far," said Boyce. "Go on."

"Point number three: the conversation Tucker overheard consisted of a few words, including 'Essex' and 'Rudd,' which, as he said, made him prick his ears up. He said he got the impression the two men were discussing a case that I'd been involved in. Then he heard a woman's name mentioned, either Milly or Molly, he wasn't sure which."

Boyce raised his shoulders and looked puzzled.

"Melly," prompted Rudd. "Melanie Thorpe. Remember?"

"Christ!" exclaimed Boyce. "That girl that was strangled? But that was four years ago!"

"Exactly," said the Inspector. "I've sent for the file to be brought up from records and we'll go over it together later on. But the point is that I'm damned sure Tucker didn't know what case the man had been referring to and I was careful not to let on that I'd realised. I just looked blank."

"I know the look," Boyce said with a grin.

Rudd returned the smile and then went on, "But why should Tucker be interested in the Thorpe case?"

"Perhaps he was just trying to be helpful?" suggested Boyce. "He's the type who'd try to keep on the good side of the law, especially if it suited him to do a little boot-licking."

"No," said Rudd positively. "It was more than that. He suggested a little too eagerly that I should look up the records and find out what case this woman had been involved in. I got the impression he was anxious to know himself. Now why?"

Boyce looked baffled.

"You've lost me there," he admitted. "But, then, Tucker's a devious little bastard. He's probably got some deep-laid motive of his own, although God knows what it could be."

"He also looked frightened at one point. It was soon after he started telling me about the conversation in the pub. He actually sweated. And you know who came into my mind, Tom? Stoll."

"Stoll?" said Boyce, sounding incredulous. "What could Stoll want with a little creep like Tucker? I know when Tucker first phoned, you thought you saw a connection between him and Stoll but, quite frankly, I don't see it myself."

"I don't see it either," Rudd admitted. "Not logically, that is. I just feel it."

"A hunch," said Boyce. He was inclined to be dismissive. "But you had a hunch Stoll would follow Tucker and you were wrong."

Rudd walked about the room, moving his shoulders restlessly; a sign, as Boyce recognised, that he was disturbed. The Sergeant nibbled his thumb-nail thoughtfully as he watched him. There were times when he wished the Inspector would give up these hunches of his and stick to solid facts. For his part, he knew what he'd do if he were in the Inspector's shoes: pull in Stoll and the Beesons for questioning. But that suggestion had already got him nowhere. Meanwhile, he couldn't think of anything constructive to say.

A knock on the door came as a welcome diversion. It was a uniformed constable bringing in a dark grey, mottled file.

"The Thorpe case, sir," he announced.

"Put it on my desk," Rudd told him.

After the constable had withdrawn, the Inspector stood looking down on its familiar mottled cover. It would all be there; the statements, the reports; sheet after sheet of typescript that told all there was to know about the death of Melanie Thorpe, except the name of her killer.

Suddenly a thought struck the Inspector. Grabbing the telephone directory, he began rapidly turning the pages, and then, having found the number he wanted, he dialled it. While it was ringing, he spoke excitedly to Boyce over the rim of the receiver.

"Who else keeps records, Tom? Newspapers! Remember how the local weekly carried the Thorpe case front-page?"

He broke off and began speaking to someone at the other end of the line. Boyce listened only intermittently. The Inspector would tell him afterwards what the outcome of the conversation had been. Meanwhile, his own thoughts returned to the Thorpe case. He remembered the girl, too; a skinny little kid. But mostly he recalled the hours of door-to-door inquiries that had gone on for months. It made his feet ache again just thinking of it.

Rudd had rung off and was looking at him with a triumphant air.

"That's one hunch that was right. Tom Someone *did* come asking to look up their back copies. But, luckily for us, the man in charge of them at the local newspaper wasn't able to oblige. It seems they no longer let people just browse among them for themselves. They've had a few copies stolen or bits torn out of them. So, the relevant copies asked for are brought down to the front office where an eye can be kept on them or, if it's someone doing more general research they ask to see some kind of bona fides, a letter of introduction or a student's membership card, something like that. The man who came asking had no letter of introduction and no idea of the date of the copies he wanted to examine. So he was told, 'Sorry, no.' "

"Tucker?" asked Boyce, looking interested.

"He described the man as well-dressed, in his thirties, pale complexioned and dark-haired."

"Stoll!" exclaimed the Sergeant.

"Exactly," said the Inspector, looking pleased with himself. "There's your connection, Tom. Tucker tells me about the case. Stoll is interested in looking up reports in the local paper. And there's an interesting time sequence as well. According to the man on the paper, he was pretty certain Stoll came in on Monday. That was four days ago. On Tuesday, Stoll starts tailing me. At least, that was the first time I noticed him. And today, Friday, Tucker rings me up and tells me about a conversation that links up with the murder of Melanie Thorpe. By the way, I've asked the man at the newspaper office not to let anyone have access to the back copies for a few days just in case Stoll tries again or sends someone in his place. But he's not keen on keeping them unavailable for too long. Someone may come genuinely wanting to look something up. So I've arranged for you to go over there tomorrow, check through the copies and remove any that refer to the Thorpe case. I'm sorry about that, Tom. It's a bit of a chore but it has to be done and, as you were on the case with me, you'll know what to look for. Incidentally, Lawson will be back some time today, bringing a copy of Stoll's photograph off his file. We know he's changed his appearance, dyed his hair and shaved off his moustache, but I'll get McCallum in the photographic department to touch it up so that it resembles Stoll as he is now. I want you to show it to a man called Hillmore on the local paper to see if he can identify it. But I'm certain in my own mind it was Stoll who called there."

"I wonder why Stoll went to the trouble to change his appearance?" Boyce asked.

Rudd lifted his shoulders indifferently.

"It's not all that important but my guess is he was counting on no-one getting more than a glimpse of him, if that. And, if we hadn't lured him into the Six Bells the other evening and got his finger-prints, we could be making inquiries about a dark, clean-shaven man, instead of a fair-haired one with a moustache. It was planned, I think, just to confuse any possible inquiries."

"Could be," agreed Boyce. "Tomorrow, then, I'll get round to the local paper. What about you?"

"I don't know," Rudd said slowly. "Although we've made a connection between Stoll and Tucker, we still haven't established why either of them should be interested in the Thorpe murder. It was a local case, Tom. It didn't even make the nationals."

"Come to that," went on Boyce, as if following his own train of thought, "we don't know yet where Stoll and Tucker met up in the first place."

"I think we can make a fair guess at that one," Rudd replied.

"Inside?"

"It seems likely. We know Stoll hadn't long finished a prison sentence in Parkgate while Tucker's been in and out of nick for years. Anyway, I've rung records at the Yard and they'll be phoning me back sometime this morning with the information on Bibby's file, so we'll know soon enough. Meanwhile, I suggest we start going over the Thorpe case to see if there's any possible clue in it as to why Tucker and Stoll should be so interested."

Boyce lifted his eyes in horror at the idea. He hated paperwork. Rudd laughed.

"Come on! It must be done. I'm sure there's some connection. I suggest we work systematically, taking the reports from the experts first; the forensic and path. stuff, and go on from there."

They were part way through them when the telephone rang. It was the call Rudd had been expecting from Records at the Yard. A bored, official voice began reading out the information.

"Donald Franklin Tucker, born May 2, 1921, height . . ."

"You can skip all that," Rudd told him firmly. "I know what he looks like, and I know something of his past record. What I want is something more recent."

"How recent?" asked the voice, sounding human.

Rudd thought quickly. Stoll had just finished serving a two-year sentence. It seemed a good point in time to pick up Bibby's career.

"The last two years?" he suggested.

"Hang on," said the voice. "I'll have a look. There's pages of it here."

There was a pause in which Rudd fancied he could hear paper rustling, then the voice came back on the line.

"Two years ago he was going straight. At least he hadn't been caught."

"Oh," said Rudd. He was disappointed. It looked as if a promising idea was going to come to nothing.

"But a year later he was inside again on a forgery and theft charge, for drawing money on someone else's post-office savings book. The sum involved wasn't much, about twenty quid, but he got twelve months, presumably because of his previous convictions. There's quite a list of them."

"And the prison he went to?" asked Rudd, although he thought he already knew the answer.

"Parkgate," said the man, which was exactly what Rudd was expecting him to say.

"And, as a matter of interest, when was he discharged?" he asked.

"Let me see," the voice said. "Ah, here it is. Quite recently, in fact. On March 3 of this year. Just under a week ago."

"Thanks," said Rudd and, ringing off, turned to Boyce.

"Tucker was in Parkgate as we thought. But the interesting thing is, Tom, he only got out six days ago."

"Well?" asked Boyce. He had planted a heavy forefinger in the middle of the typewritten page he was reading in order not to lose his place.

"Don't you see? Stoll gets discharged in January, Tucker not until six days ago. Stoll starts making inquiries at the local newspaper four days ago and tails me the following day. It's another bit added to our time sequence and it suggests to me that Stoll was waiting for Tucker to be discharged from prison before trying to follow up the Thorpe case. Now, the obvious conclusion from that is, Tucker knows me; therefore, Stoll was using him as a contact to get to me. And there's another point still. Tucker told me he overheard that conversation about a couple of months ago. Admittedly he could have been lying about the whole thing. He certainly seemed a bit put out when I asked him the date and had to stall to give himself time to think. But I reckon it was because the locale was wrong and he knew

it. It wasn't a pub at all. It couldn't have been. Tucker
was in Parkgate two months ago. Therefore he must have
overheard it inside the nick."

"Two other prisoners having a chat?" suggested Boyce.

"That's my guess," agreed the Inspector. "And one of
them, at least, must have known something about the
Thorpe murder. You know, Tom, it's possible it was the
man who killed her. I hope to God it is. I shan't rest until
I've found him and can close this case. Quite apart from
the question of justice, I hate leaving any loose ends. Anyway, I think I'll go along to Parkgate and have a chat
with the Governor. He may be able to tell us who Stoll and
Tucker associated with. Or, if that doesn't help, we can at
least get a full list of everyone inside the prison at the
same time they were serving their sentences."

"Rather you than me," said Boyce. "I know Parkgate's
not one of the really big nicks but, all the same, it must
have at least four hundred men in it doing time. That's a
hell of a lot of names to check on."

He looked suddenly gloomy.

"But I suppose I'd come in for most of that."

"Let's hope it doesn't get that far," Rudd assured him.
"With any luck, the Governor may be able to give us a list
of just a few likely people. I'll ring him and arrange to go
over there on Monday. It's only in Middlesex so I ought to
get it sorted in one day."

"Meanwhile we go on checking this lot?" asked Boyce,
pointing a finger at the file of reports.

"I'm afraid so," Rudd replied.

They read in silence for about an hour and a half and
then made a break during which Rudd sent out for tea. As
they drank it, Boyce voiced a thought that had already
passed through the Inspector's mind.

"Funny how going over an old case like this one you
remember details that seemed important at the time but
you'd forgotten; things like the path. report on the approximate time of death and the contents of the stomach. According to the experts, she died at about 8 P.M. after a
meal consisting of sardines on toast and several cups of tea.
Makes it all seem pathetic, somehow."

Rudd have him a look of quick understanding and sympathy. At times like this, he felt very close to the burly

Sergeant. However, before he could make any reply, the telephone rang again. It was Kyle.

"I'm in London, sir," he announced. "Fulham, to be exact. I followed Tucker back to an address in the area. Shall I give it to you now or wait until I report in?"

"I might as well have it now," Rudd replied, reaching for a pencil.

"It's Forty-eight Meredith Gardens. I know it sounds grand, but in fact it's a shabby street, full of houses let off mainly into furnished rooms. There's a newsagent's on the corner where I made a few discreet inquiries. Number Forty-eight is a lodging house. I hung about for half an hour or so but as Tucker didn't reappear, I assume he lives there. Do you want me to keep up the surveillance?"

"No, there's no need," Rudd replied. "You can report back. Thanks for the address."

It was useful to have, Rudd thought, as he rang off; not that he expected Bibby would stay there all that long. Knowing something of his habits, he'd probably be on the move again soon, to some other equally shabby furnished room. But, at least, if Rudd needed him, he had the telephone number of the cafe that Tucker had given him. Just to check, he rang it now. A cockney voice at the other end announced, "The Albion Caff."

"Sorry, wrong number," said Rudd and put the receiver down, smiling. That part of Bibby's story appeared to be true, if nothing much else did.

Meanwhile, Boyce, who had resumed his reading, put a pile of papers aside with a sigh.

"That's all the expert stuff checked over," he said. "Not that there's any useful leads in it, as far as I can see. So we're left with the statements we took from the other people concerned, family, friends, etc. etc."

"I want a list of names," Rudd told him.

The Sergeant raised his eyebrows.

"All of them?" he asked.

"Yes, everybody we interviewed."

"But, Christ there were hundreds of them," Boyce protested. It was an exaggeration but not all that far out. "People in the village. Known friends and acquaintances. The girls she worked with at the hairdresser's. The bus conductors and the other passengers on the buses she caught that day . . ."

"I know," said Rudd, "and I'm sorry, Tom. But we still haven't solved the basic question in this case: Why should Stoll be following me about? As I said to you before, I think I'm supposed to lead him to some person or place. At least, we're a bit further on with that now. We know it's got something to do with the murder of Melanie Thorpe. So I want a list of everybody connected with it. I'll deal with the places."

He paused. An intention had been growing in his mind that he was half ashamed to admit to the Sergeant. No, he decided, not ashamed of but self-conscious about. It was something in the nature of a pilgrimage, a return to the places that he had visited in the course of the murder inquiry four years before in order to appease some emotional and irrational desire within himself to put Melanie Thorpe's small, pale ghost into its rightful setting. But Boyce wouldn't understand it if he explained it in those terms. He would have to put it some other way, to make it seem a sensible and reasonable course of action.

"I was thinking of going over the same route Melanie Thorpe took on the day she died," he said. That way, it sounded practical rather than sentimental. "Something might come out of it."

To his relief, Boyce seemed to accept it as quite a rational idea.

"I suppose it could," he replied, "although the scent's bound to be cold by this time."

"Never mind," Rudd said. "I may turn up something we missed."

"I can't think what," Boyce remarked, indicating the pile of reports with a gesture of disgust. "We seemed to cover everything at the time. But all the same, it's worth a try, I suppose. When were you thinking of doing it?"

"Tomorrow," Rudd said. "Meanwhile you can deal with the local paper and carry on making the list of names."

"What about Stoll?" Boyce asked. "You're not proposing letting him follow you over the route?"

This thought had already occurred to Rudd, although he hadn't yet worked it out in any detail.

"I'll have to get rid of him somehow. Short of arresting him on a loitering charge, which I don't want to do, can you think of any way we could shake him off?"

Boyce gave the matter serious consideration.

"Someone passing himself off as you," he suggested. "Wearing your coat and driving your car?"

"That might work," agreed Rudd. "Stoll never follows too close and when he parks, he takes care to keep at a distance. He never gets near enough to get a good look at me. Who've we got on the force who's roughly my size and build?"

"Miller?" Boyce said. "He's about your age, too. The hair colour's different, but if we did a quick disguise job on him, using a wig, I don't think Stoll would notice from a distance."

"Right, Miller it is. I'll brief him later. But I don't want to set up anything too elaborate, so let's try to think up something simple. Now, if Stoll keeps to his usual pattern, he'll follow me home tonight. He usually parks up the road outside the maisonettes and waits until the lights have gone out in my house before driving off, back to the Beesons', as we now know. Supposing we had Miller planted at the house before I arrive? He stays the night and, tomorrow morning, sets off driving my car back here to the office. If it succeeds, Stoll will follow him and will keep watch on the car-park and the front entrance, the same as he always does. That gets him off my tail while I go over the route Melanie Thorpe took on the day she died."

Boyce pondered this, pulling at his lower lip.

"There's one difficulty you haven't thought of," he pointed out. "If Miller takes your car, what are you going to use?"

"That's easily settled," Rudd replied. "Miller drives over to my house and leaves his car for me to use tomorrow; not outside the house, of course. That would look too suspicious. But there's a garage in the main road not far away where I usually go for petrol. I know the manager and I'm sure he wouldn't mind if Miller parks his car overnight on the fore-court. Then tomorrow morning, when Miller's left with Stoll following him, I simply walk round to the garage and pick up his car. How does that strike you, Tom?"

"It sounds foolproof," Boyce admitted. "But there is one other small point perhaps we ought to think about." He looked embarrassed. "What about your sister? Might not the neighbours start talking if a strange man arrives there this afternoon and then leaves tomorrow morning, pretending to be you? You know what people are like for gossiping."

"I agree," said Rudd, "and thanks for mentioning it. It hadn't occurred to me. I don't think Dorothy will mind. After all, Miller arriving this afternoon could be a cousin or someone about the insurance. And she won't be expected to spend the night alone with a man she doesn't know. I'll be there. As for tomorrow, we can only hope that, if the neighbours see Miller, they'll assume he's me, if they happen to be looking. After all, he's only going to walk from the front door to the garage. I can't see it need cause any problems."

He looked at his watch and pulled a face.

"Look, Boyce, time's pressing. We must get this idea off the ground as soon as possible. You round Miller up and bring him to my office. See if you can fit him up with a wig of my hair colouring while you're at it. Meanwhile, I'll phone my sister and the garage."

When Boyce had gone, Rudd put through the two calls. The garage proprietor was only too pleased to oblige by letting Rudd's friend park his car overnight on his forecourt. Rudd was a regular customer and, besides, the garage owner had guessed he was in the police force. As far as he was concerned, it wouldn't be a bad thing to be in the position of doing the law a good turn.

As for Dorothy, Rudd's sister, she raised no objections, as he had anticipated, agreeing to get the spare bedroom ready for an overnight guest. He didn't go into further details at that stage. There was no need. He could explain the little she needed to know later and, knowing her, she wasn't likely to ask too many questions.

"Mr. Miller should be arriving fairly soon," he told her, before ringing off.

Boyce entered the office, accompanied by Miller, wearing a brown wig that approximated Rudd's own colouring. The Inspector made him put on his own overcoat and stand a little way off, at the far side of the office, while Rudd and Boyce looked him over critically.

"What do you think?" Rudd asked. "Could he pass for me at a distance?"

"I think so," Boyce said.

"Turn round," Rudd told Miller. "Walk about a bit."

The man did so, looking a little self-conscious.

"The build and height's right," Rudd admitted. "But what about the walk, Tom? Does that look like mine?"

"He needs to hump his shoulders more," Boyce replied.

Rudd burst out laughing, in which the two other men joined.

"Thanks very much for the compliment," he told Boyce. "Go on, Miller, hump yourself, like I do."

Grinning, Miller humped.

"That's better," Boyce said. "He's the spitting image, now; spitting enough, anyway, to fool Stoll."

"Right," said Rudd to Miller. "You'll do. Now this is the plan."

After he had explained it to Miller, he added, "Leave your car on the fore-court of Simpson's garage, in the main road. I've arranged for you to do that. And don't forget to take the wig with you. You'll need it tomorrow morning. Now, are there any questions that you'd like to ask?"

"Only one point, sir. If I'm to spend the night at your house, should I go home first and pack a few things?"

"No, don't bother," Rudd replied. "You can borrow a spare pair of my pyjamas and I don't suppose you'll mind using my electric shaver for once. As for a tooth-brush, you can pick one up on the way. It can go down on your expense sheet. But I'd rather you didn't arrive at my place carrying a bag." He looked at Boyce and winked. "The Sergeant thinks the neighbours might talk. Now, if that's all, you'd better push off straightaway. You've got my address and my sister's expecting you. Tell her I'll be home later."

After Miller had left, the Inspector and Boyce settled down again to read the reports in the Thorpe file. After a few heavy, preliminary sighs, Boyce began work on drawing up the list of names connected with the case, while Rudd wrote down the times of the known movements of the girl on the day she died.

He already recalled the main facts. It had been a Sunday in early April. Melanie had left her home in the village of Wiston to visit her father in another village, Merestead, fifteen miles away on the Essex coast. Her parents had been divorced about five years before, when Melanie had been ten. Her mother had subsequently married a local

builder, named Bridges, and settled down in the village of
Wiston with her new husband. A child, Melanie's half-
brother, was later born to them.

Melanie appeared quite happy living with her mother,
step-father and new brother. As far as Rudd could find out,
there had been no friction. But, as she got older and more
independent, she had begun visiting her father in the old
home at Merestead, going to see him by bus on a Sunday
about once a month.

Naturally, during the course of the investigation at the
time of her murder, Rudd had interviewed the father.
Thorpe was, in his opinion, a bit of a bad lot, and Mrs.
Bridges, his ex-wife, certainly seemed glad to have parted
company with him. But evidently Melanie had preserved
some affection for him, although Rudd had the impression
Mrs. Bridges didn't exactly approve of these visits. "But
then," as she had said, "He's her father, after all."

Melanie had arrived safely at Merestead, spent the day
with Thorpe in his cottage and started for home. Somewhere along that homeward journey she had met her
death.

He jotted down the time-table, as far as he had been
able to ascertain it during the first inquiries.

10:10 A.M. Caught bus in Wiston.

10:35 A.M. Got off bus at Hadley Corner and waited for
the Merestead bus.

10:50 A.M. Caught bus to Merestead.

11:25 A.M. Arrived at Merestead.

After that, the time-table became less definite, although
he had been able to establish a few facts with some accu-
racy.

1:00 P.M. approximately, had lunch in company with
her father.

6:15 P.M. approximately, had tea in company with her
father.

6:50 P.M. Caught bus back to Hadley Corner.

7:35 P.M. Got off bus at Hadley Corner.

And there the trail stopped. She should have caught the
bus for Wiston that arrived at Hadley Corner a quarter of
an hour later. But she never caught it. She was last seen
alive by the conductor of the Merestead bus, as his vehicle
pulled away, waiting at the bus stop for her next connection. It was already getting dusk by then. The place was

a country road, with very little traffic on it, especially on a
Sunday evening. The next morning, her body had been discovered half a mile up the road behind a hedge.

A few facts jotted down on a piece of paper and an overwhelming urge to make a pilgrimage. Even Rudd had to
admit the two didn't quite add up. But, all the same, tomorrow he'd find himself going over the same route the
girl had taken four years before.

Folding the piece of paper and putting it away in his
pocket, he said to Boyce, "Home, Tom?"

Boyce accepted the suggestion with alacrity. Putting on
their coats and switching off the lights, they left the office.

As Rudd had expected, Stoll in the blue mini dropped
into place a little distance behind him in the home-going
traffic. But it didn't matter any more. Miller was lined up
ready, the plan would go through. Tomorrow Stoll would
be ditched and Rudd would be free to make his pilgrimage
alone.

5

The ruse worked perfectly. The following morning, Miller, wearing Rudd's overcoat and the brown wig, got into the Inspector's car and drove off down the road, Stoll tailing him at his usual discreet distance. Rudd gave them plenty of start and then, having walked round the corner to the garage where he picked up Miller's car, he set off for Wiston.

It was a cool, blue, clear morning, no longer damp or overcast. The sky had a pale, washed-out look to it. So far the spring hadn't properly arrived. The countryside still had the barren prospect of winter about it; the trees bare, the grass rusty; the old, dead growth of last year's summer still poking out of the ditches and hedgerows; the tall, dry stalks of cows' parsley and withered bracken; the twisted coils of brambles, looking like barbed wire left over from some long-ago war. And yet, there was a sense of new life beginning. Celandines grew here and there along the grass verges, little dabs of bright yellow. The very air seemed to have life to it.

Rudd drove slowly, occasionally glancing at his watch. He had plenty of time. For some ridiculous reason that he would not have explained, he wanted to start at the exact place and at the exact time that Melanie Thorpe had begun her last journey. It seemed a point of honour to do so.

The village of Wiston hadn't changed since the last time he had been there. It was an ordinary place. No tourist, passing through it, would give it a second look. It boasted no thatched or timbered cottages, just ordinary brick houses of no particular age or beauty, and a row of new bungalows with roofs of bright red tiles. Melanie's mother lived in one of them: Ivanhoe. He remembered her weeping in the sitting-room, among the patterned cretonne and the Ercol easy chairs.

The bus stop was further down on the other side of the road. Rudd glanced again at his watch. It was ten past ten. For a moment, he half expected the green single-decker country bus to come up the road and then he remembered it was Saturday. Melanie's journey had taken place on a Sunday when a different time-table operated.

Driving along the route it had taken, he recalled some of the witnesses' statements of that first part of the bus ride. She had been alone. She had sat alone. She had spoken to nobody.

At Hadley Corner, he pulled off the road and waited. It was a T junction, miles from anywhere, with only the bus stops sticking up out of the grass verges on either side of the road, and a couple of farm cottages a hundred yards further on. He had already passed and deliberately not looked at the place where her body had been found. That would come later.

It was here she had to change buses. The bus from Wiston turned left, taking the route that finally led inland to Boxleigh, the small country town where she had worked. So the first part of the journey had been familiar to her, almost a daily routine.

She had stood at the road-side waiting for the next bus, another single-decker, which covered the route that took her to Merestead, and then went on to Tolquay and other small towns and villages along the coast. It had arrived at 10:50 A.M., which meant she had to wait a quarter of an hour. Again, witnesses on the Merestead bus had testified that she had been alone.

At the time the bus would have arrived, Rudd drove on again, following its route. It was a circuitous one. The road wound to and fro between small villages and clusters of houses, but moving always, however gradually, towards the sea. The countryside began to change subtly. The more wooded landscape of the inland farms, with their small, safe fields, neatly hedged, gave way to a broader view of flat, open countryside, with occasional far-off glimpses of water that came closer as he drew nearer to the village of Merestead. The sky widened until it took up nearly three quarters of the vista, the pale, flat expanse of it extending down and down until, at last, it reached the rim of the marshes, stretching out to meet the sea. It was a bleak, empty landscape in which the occasional tree stood out unexpectedly like an exclamation mark, and yet it had a drama and beauty of its own.

As he entered Merestead, the view vanished. It was a small, tight village in which the houses and gardens clustered closely together, as if protecting themselves from the bitter winds that blew in from the North Sea across the saltings. Parking the car and getting out, Rudd was aware of a change in the scent of the air. It no longer had the rural smell of the inland farms. There was a tang of salt in it and the odour of marshes and river mud.

Thorpe's cottage was one of a pair set behind the main cluster of houses, down a little lane. As he approached it, he wondered what he would say to the man to account for his visit. Fresh information has come our way which makes it necessary to reopen inquiries? Probably something like that. Interviewing the relatives of the dead was the one aspect of his work that he had never fully come to terms with. He found it easier to take refuge behind the unemotional, stilted phrases of official language.

He remembered how Thorpe had taken the news of his daughter's death. Grief had made him angry and bitter. It had suddenly occurred to Rudd that the man had no-one left. He was now totally alone.

It came as a shock to the Inspector to find the cottages empty and derelict, the windows boarded over. Even the paths up to the front doors had disappeared among the wilderness of the overgrown gardens. Pausing at the gate, he looked at them. It was clear what must have happened. Four years ago, when Thorpe had lived there, they had been badly dilapidated. Since then they must have been declared unfit for habitation and their occupants moved out elsewhere.

All the same, he lingered at the gate. It was the place where Melanie had spent the last day of her life. He remembered the squalor of Thorpe's cottage, the curtains rotting at the windows, the table littered with dirty crockery, beer bottles in the fireplace, a smell of mice and decay. It had occurred to him then how different Mrs. Bridges' life must be in her trim, modern bungalow, although, no doubt, the cottage had been properly looked after when she was married to Thorpe. During the first inquiries, Rudd had picked up some interesting bits of gossip about them. Thorpe had been caught with a woman from some caravans that had moved into the neighbourhood and parked on a piece of waste-land. Gipsies, the gossip had said, but Rudd doubted if they were real Romanies. More likely tinkers, or what East Anglian people call "did-decoys." Anyway, she had left him, taking Melanie with her, and sued for divorce. He got the impression it had been a relief to her to be rid of the man. And yet Melanie had come back, trying to fulfill, in some small way, the role her mother had played. The time she had spent in the cottage on that day seemed to have been taken up with household chores, an attempt, no doubt, to bring some order into the squalor of her father's existence. Thorpe himself had been vague about what precisely she had done in the seven hours she had been with him. They had talked for a while. She had prepared the meals and cleared up afterwards. She had done some washing and probably tried cleaning the floors. The next-door neighbour had noticed shirts pegged out to dry on the line in the back garden and had seen her emptying a bucket of dirty water down the outside drain.

Thorpe had mourned for her in his own bitter, angry way. Rudd remembered him banging the table with his fist, making the dirty plates and cups on it jump and rattle, while the dog, a sad, white mongrel, looked on, frightened.

Rudd had forgotten the dog until that moment. It had been one of those abject creatures, lying quietly in a corner of the room most of the time, hardly making its presence known. Not that Rudd got the impression that Thorpe ill-used it physically. He seemed to ignore it, although it followed him about patiently at his heels. The Inspector couldn't remember what it was called, or if indeed it had a name.

Rousing himself, he turned away from his contemplation of the cottages. He would have to find out where Thorpe was now living and the most likely place to ask was the village shop.

The woman who ran it was inclined to be disobliging.

"Thorpe?" she asked sharply. Rudd realised she didn't

like the man and some of her hostility was directed at him-self for inquiring about him. "He's most likely to be at the Anchor."

"But where is he living now?" Rudd persisted.

She hesitated as if unwilling to appear she knew any-thing about him.

"I need to find him," Rudd added.

She relented, although ungraciously.

"He's got an old house-boat down on the marshes. Fol-low the sea-wall round to the left and you'll find it."

He thanked her and departed.

The Anchor was a little further on down the village. Rudd stuck his head round the doors of both bars but there was no sign of Thorpe in either of them. Turning away, he set off for the far end of the village. Here the houses grad-ually petered out, giving place to a few tumble-down boat-sheds, and beyond these the saltings took over. On this part of the coast, the sea comes sweeping up in great arms of water that divide into creeks, some large enough to be nav-igable, some no wider than ditches that at low tide are mere empty channels; narrow tentacles that creep inland through the sour, coarse marsh grass and the clumps of sea-blite. It is a coast that attracts few casual visitors, even in summer, for there are none of the delights of the sandy beaches and amusement arcades of sea-side resorts, al-though specialists, yachtsmen and men interested in fishing and wild-fowling, come to it. But it is not the place for the amateur. The currents and mud-banks off-shore make sail-ing hazardous, and the tide, creeping quietly in across the marshes, can cut a man off for hours, if not actually drowning him. Some of the coastal villages had become yachting centres but Merestead was not one of them. The inlet on which it was situated had silted up and was too shallow for sailing, although a few rowing-boats, pulled up on the muddy fore-shore, suggested that some of the local men might go lobster or crab fishing in their spare time.

Rough wooden steps led up to the top of the sea-wall that ran straight for a short distance and then turned in-land towards the lusher water meadows. Rudd followed the narrow path along its top. To his right lay the marshes and beyond them the sea, shining dully like pewter. The tide was running out and the mud-flats were emerging, showing their own complex geography of banks and channels, strewn with the debris left behind by the receding water: sea-weed and crabs and pieces of sodden timber with, here and there, the carcase of some derelict, abandoned boat, half buried in the mud, only its ribs sticking out above the silt.

He had been walking for about ten minutes when he came to Thorpe's house-boat. It was tied up in the creek that ran alongside the dyke, almost level with its top, although, as the tide went further out, it would drop lower in the water. It was an extraordinary craft. Rudd, who knew little about boats, guessed it had been converted from a lifeboat. Decking a few feet wide had been laid across it fore and aft, but most of it was covered over with a roughly built super-structure resembling a hen-house that someone, unskilled in carpentry, had knocked together in a few spare hours. It had a low door in it and a couple of windows, the walls and roof being clad with tarred paper. An iron stove pipe protruded from the roof. It was moored to stakes driven into the sea-wall and there no doubt it would remain, quietly rotting over the years.

It was the air of decay about it that made Rudd certain it was the boat where Thorpe was now living, even before he noticed the dog curled up asleep on the decking. It woke as he approached but didn't bark, merely making a low, whining noise in its throat. Rudd remembered this had been one of the creature's characteristics: its almost total silence. Scrambling ashore, it sidled up to him, keeping its rump low, expecting to be rebuffed but hoping for some attention. Rudd patted its head, at the same time trying to keep it away from his trouser legs, recalling how the chairs and the matting in Thorpe's cottage had been coated with its white hairs.

Thorpe had evidently also heard the Inspector's approach; perhaps the dog's whining had alerted him. His face appeared at one of the windows and, a few seconds later, the door opened and he half emerged, asking roughly, "What do you want?"

"You remember me?" Rudd inquired, parrying Thorpe's question with one of his own.

The man looked him up and down.

"Yes," he said, without much interest.

Rudd had already noticed his appearance. Thorpe had

never taken much care of himself, but the Inspector could see he had deteriorated even further. Several days' growth of coarse, greying stubble covered his face and the open-necked shirt and old jacket he was wearing were filthy. Through a great rent in the seam of one of the shoulders the ragged lining was showing.

"I'd like a chat with you, if you can spare the time," Rudd went on. "Can I come aboard?"

As he said it, it occurred to him that "aboard" was too precise and nautical a term to use for that floating shed.

Thorpe merely lifted his shoulders, an indifferent gesture that the Inspector took for assent. Getting aboard, however, was a more difficult operation than he had imagined. A series of crude steps, little more than ledges, had been cut into the dyke bank, evidently for use at low tide when the boat would be lying well below the level of the sea-wall. With the tide on the turn, the sill of the door was only a matter of some eighteen inches away but it was an awkward step to take down from the narrow path on which he was standing to the low door opening.

Rudd made it in an ungainly scramble that Thorpe watched with sour amusement. From the door-sill there was another step down into the interior of the boat itself. He arrived, a little out of breath, with his jacket sleeves riding up his arms. As he pulled them down, he looked about him with quick interest.

It was larger inside than he had imagined, for the wooden super-structure had given the boat a squat, top-heavy look. It was about twenty-six feet long, he reckoned, divided into two parts by a curtain that was pulled to one side. The part in which he was standing had been roughly converted into a living-area. A two-burner oil stove stood on a bench with a sink beside it let into the same working top. Opposite ran another bench, lower and topped by a sheet of dirty foam-rubber, which evidently served as seating, and in one corner was a small, round, coke-burning stove the chimney of which he had seen sticking out of the roof.

Beyond the curtain was a sleeping-area that contained two bunk beds, one of which was piled up with clothes and other gear. An oil lamp hung from a hook in the ceiling, which Rudd nearly banged his head on as he came in. Otherwise there was just sufficient head-room for him to stand upright.

No attempt had been made to cover in the structure of the hull, the iron framework of which was still exposed, with its round bolt-heads showing, and everywhere was painted a dingy battleship grey that added to the general appearance of dismal squalor. Clothes, dirty crockery, empty tins, half-used bottles of milk littered the place, together with an unusual number of plastic containers that puzzled Rudd at first, until he realised Thorpe would use them to bring drinking water from the village. A pair of wellington boots, their tops turned down, lay abandoned in the centre of the cabin. Thorpe kicked them to one side.

"Well?" he demanded with a sullen air.

"Mind if I sit down?" Rudd replied pleasantly. "I'm a bit puffed from scrambling down that sea-wall."

He sat before Thorpe had time to reply and then blew his nose. The air in the place stank of paraffin oil, sour milk, and old dog, a complex odour that caught him at the back of the throat.

"What are you here for?" Thorpe asked. Some of the fight had gone out of him in the face of Rudd's equanimity. He was uneasy, uncertain what to make of the Inspector's presence and, Rudd felt, ashamed as well, although of what he was not sure. Perhaps that Rudd should see the degradation and squalor to which he had finally descended? It seemed unlikely. It was, in fact, in not much worse state than the cottage, although, being confined to a smaller space, it appeared so.

"Fresh infor . . ." began Rudd and then stopped. He couldn't use that ridiculous, formal phrase; not here, among the dirt and the stench.

He started again.

"Your daughter . . ."

Thorpe interrupted him fiercely, regaining a little of his former belligerence.

"What about her?"

"Mr. Thorpe," Rudd said patiently, "I'm not here to cause any trouble for you. But you must realise the case on your daughter was never closed. For reasons I can't explain, I've got to ask a few more questions."

"You've got the bloke what killed her?"

There was a terrible eagerness in Thorpe's voice and expression. Rudd saw his hands grip into fists.

"Nothing as definite as that," he replied. "Just a small piece of information that may mean nothing much. But I have to follow it up. You see that, don't you?"

As he was speaking, Thorpe watched his face with a listening intensity, following the movements of the Inspector's lips as if he were deaf. Finally, he nodded, indicating that he had taken in what Rudd had said.

"I need to go over again what Melly did on the last day she visited the cottage," Rudd went on. He deliberately used the pet name which she had been called by the family, knowing it would make Thorpe more vulnerable.

The man turned his face away.

"She arrived on the bus at about half-past eleven?" Rudd prompted him gently.

Thorpe merely moved his head in assent.

"And then what happened?"

"It's four years ago," Thorpe began.

"It's important that you try to remember, Mr. Thorpe."

"I told you all I could at the time."

"You talked for a time?"

There was a silence and then Thorpe said, "Yes. She made a pot of tea and we sat drinking it."

"What did you talk about?"

It was like probing into a wound. At each question, Thorpe flinched as if in physical pain.

"Christ, what do you talk about? The weather. The garden. How she was getting on at work."

Not, Rudd guessed, about her mother or her step-father.

"And then?"

"I dunno. She cleared up a bit. I didn't pay much mind. It were woman's work. I heard her out in the kitchen."

It was a long statement for Thorpe.

"That kept her busy until you had dinner?"

"Yes."

"And after you had eaten?"

"I dunno, I tell you. She washed up. She were still at it, clearing up. I remember she come through to sweep the floor."

There was something odd about the construction of this last sentence that Rudd couldn't exactly analyse, although perhaps the strangeness of it lay more in Thorpe's manner of saying it than in the words themselves. He was on the defensive again, uneasy.

Rudd pounced, although on what he wasn't himself sure. "Through?" he said sharply. "From the kitchen you mean?"

But the impression had gone, like a quick shadow. Thorpe merely shrugged. "I reckon so. She was out there," he replied.

Washing up. Washing clothes. Washing the floor.

"And then she got tea," Thorpe added, without any prompting.

That seemed to be the end of it. Not long afterwards, Melanie had walked to the village to catch the bus back to Hadley Corner. Yet Rudd went on sitting. There was still something unsatisfactory about Thorpe's statement that Rudd had felt the first time he interviewed him. Even allowing for the fact that he wasn't very articulate, that he had a natural dislike of talking about his murdered daughter and an antipathy towards the police anyway, there was a lack of communication that rose from some other reluctance that Rudd couldn't put his finger on.

Thorpe was saying, "Look, if that's all, I want to get myself something to eat."

It was clear he wanted Rudd to go. The Inspector rose to his feet.

"Thank you, Mr. Thorpe," he said, using the official formula as some kind of cover of his own. "I'm sorry I've had to take up your time."

He ducked out of the doorway and scrambled up the bank, taking it in two strides this time as the boat was lying appreciably lower in the water. As he reached the dyke path. Thorpe shouted after him:

"You'll tell me when you get him?"

Presumably he meant his daughter's murderer.

"I'll keep you informed," Rudd told him.

He noticed the white mongrel had risen to its feet on the tiny area of after-decking and was wagging its tail feebly as if in anticipation of some treat but, seeing it was only Rudd departing, it lay down again, resting its chin mournfully on its fore-paws.

Rudd walked back to the village. The tide had slipped

further out, revealing more of the mud-flats. He could hear the water gurgling and sucking in the channels, and the mournful, high cry of sea-birds, sounding lost and alone.

The public bar of the Anchor was a little more cheerful. Rudd went to the counter and ordered a pint of bitter, placing himself deliberately near the landlady so that she would serve him. Women gossiped more easily than men.

"Mr. Thorpe not in yet?" he asked as she passed the glass across to him.

She glanced at the clock on the wall.

"Not yet," she replied. "He'll be in later."

"Oh," said Rudd, looking disappointed. "I was hoping to catch him. I asked at the garage but he wasn't there."

Four years before, Thorpe had been employed at the local garage mainly, Rudd gathered, as a petrol-pump attendant as he hadn't much skill as a mechanic.

The lie worked.

"Got the push," the woman replied.

"Oh?" said Rudd, this time with interest, leaning one elbow on the bar, inviting her co-operation.

"A bit too much of the . . ." She completed the sentence with several quick movements of her right hand, indicating drinking. Then her attention sharpened. She was no fool.

"Haven't I seen you somewhere before?" she asked.

Rudd doubted if she would connect him with the Thorpe murder inquiries after all these years. Boyce and others had been concerned with the door-to-door questioning in the village, including the Anchor, where Thorpe's statement that he hadn't been to the pub that mid-day had been checked. Rudd had done nothing more than call in to pick up Boyce one lunch-time. But her suspicions were aroused and she was clearly disinclined to say anything more.

"I'm around the district from time to time," he said vaguely and retreated from the situation by carrying his pint of beer over to a table. The scrap of gossip, however, was interesting. If Thorpe had been sacked from the garage, Rudd wondered what he did for money. There was always the dole, of course, and his life-style was simple. Perhaps he picked up a little extra by doing casual work on the farms in the area.

Before he left, he caught the landlady's attention.

"Don't tell Mr. Thorpe I was asking for him," he said.

He dropped an eyelid in a conspiratorial wink, letting her interpret it as she wished. She gave him a glare.

"Don't worry," she told him. "I don't speak to the man unless I have to."

Rudd emerged from the pub, feeling well-pleased at this little encounter. It had been an amusing interlude in an otherwise unrewarding and depressing day.

Driving on to the next village, he treated himself to a ploughman's lunch of bread, cheese and pickle, and another pint, at the Red Lion, taking his time over it before driving slowly back to Merestead, parking the car where he could watch the Anchor without being seen himself.

At three o'clock closing time, Thorpe came out, the dog at his heels, and made for the far end of the village, walking with the deliberate and careful gait of a man who has had too much to drink but is not quite staggering drunk.

Rudd waited and then followed him on foot at a distance.

When he came to the wooden steps leading to the top of the sea-wall, Thorpe hoisted himself up them heavily, tread by tread, pausing at the top, to get breath and regain his balance. Then he set off slowly along the dyke path, the dog following humbly a little way behind, stopping when he stopped, moving on when he did.

Rudd watched them for several minutes. Despite the narrowness of the path and the steep drop on either side, Thorpe seemed in no way unsure on his feet. No doubt, he had made the same journey in the same manner many times before.

Thoughtfully, the Inspector turned away and walked back to the car.

6

Still driving slowly, he went back over the route he had already covered, to Hadley Corner, passing on his right-hand side the bus stop where Melanie Thorpe had waited, after getting off the bus from Merestead at twenty-five minutes to eight, the last time she had been seen alive.

As he drove past it, he gave it a quick glance. At that point along the grass verge someone, some man, had stopped and offered her a lift, if Rudd's theory was correct.

About half a mile further on was the gate opening to a field, in which her body had been found.

Slowing down, he drew the car off the road into the opening as her murderer must have done. It was wide enough to take a car, deeply rutted, as it had been on that day four years before, by the thick tread of tractor tyres that passed through it to the field beyond. For a few minutes, he remained quietly at the wheel. The pilgrimage was almost over. But there was only so much room for sentiment and memories. Facts were what mattered and he went over in his mind the evidence that the forensic experts had discovered about the manner in which Melanie Thorpe had met her death.

She had been strangled from behind. The position of the marks on her throat had indicated this. And strangled quickly by someone with strong hands. The attack had been unexpected, too. She hadn't anticipated it. There had been no signs of a struggle; no bruising on her face or body to suggest she had fought for her life.

Rudd mulled over again what these facts suggested. There were some curious aspects of them that, at the time of the first inquiry, hadn't quite added up, and they still didn't.

A man gives a lift to a girl. Presumably she sits beside him in the front passenger's seat. Then he draws off the road and strangles her from *behind*. At the time, Rudd had even gone so far as to re-enact it, getting a policewoman to sit beside him in his car while he tried putting his hands round her neck from the back. He had found it almost impossible to do. In that cramped space, with the steering wheel in the way, he had to twist himself uncomfortably sideways. It would certainly have been impossible to strangle anyone quickly and efficiently in that position, before she had time to put up a struggle.

The obvious inference was that Melanie Thorpe and the man had got out of the car and he had killed her as she stood with her back to him. Yet that seemed unlikely. Melanie had been a quiet girl, rather shy of boys. The manageress of the hairdresser's where she had been serving her apprenticeship had told him she was even a little timid with the women customers, rarely speaking unless they spoke first. Even if she had accepted a lift from some man she didn't know, and that in itself was out of character, it would have been even more out of character for her to get out of the car, in a gateway, on a lonely stretch of road, in company with the man, thus placing herself in an even more vulnerable position.

Rudd had concluded it was someone she knew, on however slight an acquaintance, and trusted. But exhaustive inquiries had turned up no-one in her small circle who could have fitted this description. Boyce and the other policemen on the inquiry had interviewed every man who owned a car whom she might have known, however slightly; men from Merestead, men from Wiston; men from Boxleigh, the small town where she worked; even the bus conductors who worked the route she regularly travelled; the delivery men who called at her home; her stepfather's friends and acquaintances; the salesmen in the local shops. They had been eliminated one by one from the inquiry, usually on the grounds of an alibi that accounted for their movements at the time of her death. Only a handful had remained and there had been nothing in their background or character to suggest any of them was her murderer. The lack of motive had been baffling at the time, and it still was.

But, for whatever reason, someone had killed her and then carried her body to dump it over the gate into the field beyond.

Getting out of the car, Rudd went and leaned on the top bar, looking down at the place where her body had been found. There were obvious differences. At the time, it had been a scene of busy activity, crowded with people; Rudd himself together with Boyce and the other plain-clothes detectives; the photographer; the police surgeon; the ambulance attendants; a man examining the ruts in the gate opening, hoping to pick up recent signs of a car's tyre treads and being disappointed. The ground had been too dry and hard to retain any impressions. Meanwhile, men in uniform had been searching the hedge and the grass verges for any clue, however small, that might prove useful in the investigation. The road-side had been lined with parked vehicles.

There were other subtler differences, too. It had been April then and the spring had been more advanced. The leaves on the trees and bushes were opening out, softening their twiggy sharpness. The whole landscape was gentler and greener. The wheat that was growing in the field was taller, too, and lusher. The field still grew wheat but the short stems of it were now only showing a few inches above the brown earth.

Otherwise the setting was as it had been on that day. Alongside the hedge ran a strip of uncultivated verge that the tractor had not been able to plough. It was there, on the right, among the rough grass and the young nettles, just pushing into vigorous, green growth, that Melanie's body had been found; just dumped down; flung aside like a sackful of old rubbish that no-one had any more use for.

He remembered the huddled shape that, at first sight, had seemed nothing more than a bundle of clothes. Then, a few seconds later, he had been squatting down over it, the detective in him taking over as he noted details of the exact positioning of the body, the bruises on her throat, while Boyce shouted instructions and men's feet went to and fro just beyond his line of vision, as some constables set about erecting a canvas screen.

Strangely enough, he recalled the details of her clothing from another occasion, as they were being packed up into plastic bags at headquarters for despatch to forensic for detailed examination. There had been some chain-store underwear, a fawn wool trouser suit, a blue jumper, a short, dark brown overcoat, with toggle fastenings, a pair of flat-heeled shoes and white ankle socks; none of it the fashionable gear that some teen-age girls wear; just sensible, serviceable clothing, suitable for a day out in the country.

Nothing much that was useful had come out of the forensic report. A small stain on the jacket had turned out to be nothing more sinister than gravy. But, as he leaned on the gate, thinking about it, another detail stirred faintly at the back of Rudd's mind; just a line in the report mentioning something that he couldn't quite recall for the moment. Boyce had gone over the report the day before when he had reread the Thorpe file. It was obviously something that hadn't struck the Sergeant as significant. Anyway, the file would still be in the office. Rudd could check it for himself on his return.

His own task had been to examine the report on the evidence of finger-prints. He had read it through, although he knew before he started that it contained nothing useful. Whoever the man was, he had worn gloves. Blurred smudges on the girl's hand-bag had suggested this.

That had been another puzzling feature of the case that had struck Rudd at the time of the initial investigation. The hand-bag had been found open and obviously rifled in the ditch at the side of the road, thrown carelessly aside as Melly's body had been. Someone had gone through it, presumably the man who had killed her. But why? No money had been taken, so the motive was clearly not robbery. According to her mother, she had left home with about three pounds on her and, when the bag had been found, two pound notes and some loose change were still in her purse; the correct amount, allowing for the fact that she had had to pay for bus fares. The only thing that had been missing was a key-ring in the shape of a little black cat with green glass eyes; a cheap, plastic object that could have been bought at any Woolworth's for less than fifty pence. The front-door key to which it should have been attached had been found lying loose in the bottom.

Why should anyone want to take a little trinket like that? It had seemed a worthwhile clue at the time but further inquiries had proved that it could have been inconclusive. Melanie's mother, who had given Rudd a detailed list of the contents of Melly's bag and had noticed it was missing, had later admitted that Melly could have removed the key-ring herself, even though the girl had looked on it as something of a lucky charm. It was an awkward shape to fit into her purse and she had spoken of replacing it with something smaller. Or she might have mislaid it.

Yet the man who had gone through her bag had evidently been looking for something. The fact that the bag had been found open, its contents churned over, suggested this. But, whatever it was, it was unlikely to have been a plastic key-ring.

The rest of the contents had been ordinary enough. Rudd remembered them laid out on the top of a desk in readiness for an inventory to be drawn up: lipstick, compact, comb, purse, handkerchief, key, a monthly season ticket for the bus and a six-week-old receipt for a pair of jeans she had bought in a shop in Boxleigh High Street. Rudd had even sent Boyce off to check this last item, in the hope that it might prove significant. It hadn't been. The shop was a small boutique with girl assistants only. Melanie seemed to have kept the receipt for no other reason than she had forgotten to throw it away.

Facts. But they all had to be checked, even the smallest, and none of them had led anywhere; certainly not to the identity of Melanie Thorpe's killer.

And yet, Stoll and Tucker knew something. Stoll had gone to the trouble of calling at the local newspaper office, asking to look at the files. He had then followed Rudd with a tenacious and patient persistence for four days. Tucker had travelled down specially from London to tell the Inspector about a scrap of overheard conversation. It seemed a long way to come to repeat three words: Essex, Rudd's name and a girl's name.

Rudd suddenly stood upright. No, there had been four words. Afterwards Tucker had added one more. The word "transit."

Blast! He had forgotten to mention it to Boyce. Not that it mattered all that much. He'd see Boyce when he called at the office later. Then he remembered he wouldn't be able to do so. The ruse set up to draw Stoll into following Miller would have to be set into reverse that evening. It had been agreed that Miller, still acting the part of Rudd, would drive back to Rudd's house that evening, putting the car away in the garage and letting himself in by the front door.

Rudd, meanwhile, would drive Miller's car back to the garage, leaving it on the fore-court, and walk back to his house in the interval while Stoll was circling the block, as he usually did, before returning to park near the maisonettes further up the road. Miller would then slip quietly out of the house and pick up his own car.

It was a matter of fairly careful timing that had already been worked out and agreed on. But if Rudd returned to headquarters while Stoll was still parked in the side-street watching the entrance of the building and the car-park, the chances were he'd be seen and Stoll would become suspicious.

Rudd couldn't risk it. He'd have to wait until the following day to check on the forensic report and tell Boyce about the fourth word that Tucker had mentioned.

Transit. He turned it over in his mind as he stood at the gate. It was a strange word for anyone to use in connection with a murder, although Tucker hadn't realised that it was the subject of the scrap of conversation he had overheard. It suggested transport to the Inspector's mind. Movement. Vehicles. Goods being transferred from one place to another. There had been nothing like that in the Thorpe case.

He puzzled over it for several minutes and then gave up. The obvious answer was to look it up in a dictionary. The local public library ought to have a large, detailed one that would list all the possible meanings of the word. It was another fact to be checked out later.

He glanced at his watch and realised he ought to be moving on. There was one last part of the pilgrimage to be completed before he drove back to make the substitution with Miller.

Visiting the girl's grave was pure sentiment. He gained nothing factual from standing in front of it, looking down at the neat, white headstone and kerb that had replaced the mound of earth covered with wreaths beside which he had stood when he attended her funeral.

. He had gone in his official capacity, wearing a black arm-band on the sleeve of his rain-coat, while two plainclothes men mingled anonymously with the mourners in the hope that Melanie's killer, out of some morbid or twisted curiosity, might also be present.

There had been no one suspicious. Everyone present on that occasion had been checked and were accounted for. They had been Melanie's family, neighbours, a few friends, a girl from the place where she worked, that was all.

Thorpe hadn't been there, although he had sent a wreath, the card of which bore the simple message "To Melly, from her loving Dad."

Rudd had understood his absence. No doubt he had preferred not to be present when he was certain to meet his ex-wife and her new husband face to face. The Inspector guessed what he had done instead. Probably he had gone to the Anchor, seeking his own kind of consolation.

Looking down on Melly's grave, a new thought suddenly struck him. Until now, he had been concerned with Melly's movements, what she had done on the last day of her life. His questioning of Thorpe that afternoon, and at the time of the initial inquiry, had been slanted in that direction. It hadn't occurred to him to ask in much detail what Thorpe had done with himself that day.

He hadn't made his usual lunch-time visit to the Anchor. That much was certain. Boyce had checked on it at the pub and had been given positive confirmation by the landlord and his wife, as well as the customers who had been there that Sunday. Thorpe himself had stated that he spent the day at the cottage in the company of his daughter.

What else had he said about his own movements that day? Rudd tried to recall the statements that Thorpe had made. The morning seemed to be fully accounted for. Melanie had arrived at about half-past eleven. What remained of the morning had been taken up with drinking tea, talking and eating a mid-day meal together that Melanie had prepared. After the meal, she seemed to have been busy doing household chores. But what had Thorpe done? Sat in a chair? Read the newspaper? Pottered about doing some task of his own? If they finished the meal at two o'clock, and that was allowing plenty of time in which to complete it, there was a gap of about four hours until tea-time in which Thorpe must have occupied himself in some way. He hadn't gone to the pub, so what had he done?

"I remember she come through to sweep the floor."

Thorpe's remark, which had struck Rudd as strange at the time, echoed in his mind.

He recalled the cottage as he remembered it from the

initial inquiry. It was a primitive two-up, two-down house, built of weather-boarding, with a lean-to scullery at the back that contained the sink and an oil cooker, the place where presumably Melanie had washed up and laundered the shirts that the neighbour had seen hanging on the line.

Thorpe must have been in the living-room that opened directly out of the tiny scullery. He had spoken of hearing Melly at work out there. Rudd imagined he could hear the domestic noises that he sometimes heard his own sister making at home while she worked in the kitchen: the rattle of plates being put away, water gushing from a tap, the metallic clatter as a saucepan lid was removed.

At some point, Melly had gone back into the living-room to sweep the floor. Thorpe had remembered that with an odd certainty, considering he had been so vague about her other activities, merely alluding to them as "woman's work" in a tone of voice that suggested contempt for such domestic trivialities. But why had he remembered this particular piece of housework that Melly had been engaged in?

Rudd tried to put himself in Thorpe's place to picture him in the setting of that living-room. The trouble was the more recent background against which he had seen him, the interior of the house-boat, kept intruding itself. He remembered the pair of wellington boots that Thorpe had kicked to one side and the litter of plastic containers.

He gave up. Time was pressing. He would have to start back at any minute and the circumstances weren't right to allow his memory to reconstruct this kind of detail, to recall the fleeting impressions of a moment, or to give his imagination the freedom in which to interpret them.

He needed to sit down quietly, without any sense of urgency, and to replay in his mind, so to speak, the two occasions on which he had interviewed Thorpe: in the cottage, four years ago; and today, in the house-boat; like rerunning a film through a projector for a second viewing.

Turning away, he walked back through the graveyard to where he had parked the car and drove out of Wiston.

The substitution was successfully completed, without apparently arousing Stoll's suspicious, for the next day, Sunday, he was back in his usual place, in the parking bay outside the block of maisonettes.

The Inspector saw him when he backed his car out of

the garage to clean it. He had decided not to go into the office that day but to spend it quietly at home. The public library was shut, Boyce was away himself for the day, taking his wife and children on a visit to his mother's, and it didn't seem worth the journey just to look up the detail in the forensic report, which he could do on Monday.

He had intended going over in his mind the two visits to Thorpe but, although he settled himself down quietly in his armchair in the sitting-room, his mind remained obstinately blank.

He realised the presence of two people were forming a barrier against it, inhibiting full recollection.

One was Stoll, who, although unseen from inside the house, was still present in the Inspector's consciousness. At first, he had been intrigued by the man's constant vigil, then inclined to be amused by it. Now he found, as Boyce had suggested, his continual presence was beginning to get on his nerves. Would he never be rid of him?

The other person who inhibited his memory was his sister. Although she moved quietly about the house, preparing the Sunday dinner, leaving Rudd to his own devices, he was uncomfortably aware of her presence also, but for another reason. It reminded him too much of the relationship between Thorpe and his daughter—Melly going about the household tasks that Thorpe dismissed as "woman's work." He didn't like this self-identification with the man. It made him feel guilty and ill at ease to such an extent that he helped Dorothy wash up after lunch, an offer that surprised her but which assuaged his own conscience. He doubted if Thorpe had made a similar gesture.

Otherwise, he got no closer to the man. The two interviews remained nebulous, unfixed, a series of small events and remarks that he couldn't reconstruct into anything like their original. He remembered some details: Thorpe's eagerness to get rid of him on the second visit. That, at least, clicked into place. Thorpe had wanted him out of the way in order to eat before setting off for his afternoon's drinking bout at the Anchor. A man of Thorpe's disposition wouldn't like it if this habit were to be disarranged by a visitor staying too long. For some people, it was food or sleep. They were made unhappy and uneasy if meal-times and bed-times did not keep to a regular pattern.

Apart from this one detail, nothing much else fitted together. He kept coming back to small irrelevancies. The plastic water containers in Thorpe's house-boat were an example. He knew they weren't significant in themselves but were part of a train of thought that might lead him to something that was, if only he could follow it through. He felt it had something to do with the interior of the cottage, some tiny detail that he had noticed at the time and which now escaped him. It was no good going back there. The place was boarded up. Whatever it was that he had seen would be gone now for ever.

Dorothy announced that tea was ready and he abandoned the attempt at recall. After tea, he watched television in a grumpy mood, unable to settle down again to any constructive thought.

All he could do was hope that, if it wasn't forced, the memory might return unbidden, floating up from some depth of his subconscious mind where, at the moment, it lay submerged and forgotten.

7

The following day, Monday, Rudd set off for Parkgate prison, managing to shake off Stoll by the simple method of overtaking a heavy lorry and then, under cover of its huge bulk, turning left into a net-work of side-roads. When he re-emerged into the main road several miles further on, Stoll's car, a Vauxhall this time, was no longer in sight.

Parkgate prison had been built in the hey-day of the Victorian Gothic, when architects had designed main-line stations to look like cathedrals and prisons to look like medieval castles. It had turrets, battlements and crenellations, and a huge main door, elaborately studded and strapped with iron, that wouldn't have looked out of place in the Tower of London. Rudd was admitted through a smaller, humbler wicket opening and was shown up to the Governor's office.

It was a room that held a fine balance between the official and the personal, with steel filing cabinets and chintz curtains, while on the desk were photographs of the Governor's family together with some buff-coloured folders. Through the window, Rudd had a view of the vegetable garden where a man in prison uniform, grey battle-dress top and trousers, was slowly hoeing along a row of seedlings.

The Governor, McKinley, showed the same balance of humanity and officialdom in his own personality and appearance. He had a brisk voice and manner and humorous eyes.

The two men sat down, McKinley indicating the folders on his desk.

"I've had the names drawn up; two lots, in fact; one a

72

complete list of everyone who was in the prison at the time Stoll and Tucker were serving their sentences. Some have been discharged; I've marked those with an asterisk. The others are still here. The second list is the men who were in E block with Stoll and Tucker. I've given their offences alongside the names. I don't know if you'd care to look over them now? There may be someone I can give you further details about."

As he took the folder and opened it, Rudd silently blessed McKinley for his efficiency. It was the kind of organisation that made his own job so much easier.

Glancing down the list of names, however, he saw none that seemed familiar. Nor were the offences in any way out of the ordinary for a group of men in prison. They included fraud, burglary, breaking and entering, assault, sex offences of various sorts and one blackmailer.

McKinley, who had been watching Rudd's face as he looked over the list, smiled.

"I know what you're thinking. This sort of information's quite useful in its way but it only skims the surface. I get endless pieces of paper, all of which have to be filed. I expect you find it the same. But I feel myself there's nothing to beat personal contact."

Rudd nodded with quick agreement.

"So," McKinley went on, "I've made a point of having a chat with the warders in E block. According to them, Stoll caused no trouble. On paper, he was what could be described as a model prisoner; no fuss; no complaints; no aggression. He got full remission. Yet, the interesting thing was none of them liked him. There was nothing positive in his behaviour to go on; just a subtle air of withdrawal and non-co-operation, although even that's putting it too strongly. He was negative in his attitude to them and that tended to put their backs up. He didn't mix much with the other prisoners either, although, when I asked specifically about his relationship with Tucker, one of the warders remembered seeing them talking together. It struck him a bit odd at the time. But, on the other hand, as he said, if a man's doing a two-year prison sentence, he has to talk to somebody sometime. Tucker was an entirely different proposition. Do you know him?"

"Yes," said Rudd. "I do."

"Then you'll probably know what I mean. Unlike Stoll,

he was almost pathetically eager to make friends, both with the other prisoners and the warders. In fact, it was this desire to chat up the 'screws' that got him into a bit of trouble a few months after he got here. He was in D block then. I never fully got to the bottom of what happened, although, of course, I had an inquiry made at the time. There was some sort of scuffle on the stairs and Tucker fell, badly spraining his wrist. He said he was pushed. The other men swore he lost his balance. As there had been no warder nearby at the time, we couldn't come to any definite conclusion. One of the warders told me later, however, that a prisoner's cell had been searched that morning and a quantity of tobacco found. Tucker had, in fact, tipped off the warder in an attempt to ingratiate himself, and the other prisoners, realising this, had taken their own revenge on him for grassing. Anyway, he spent a week in the prison hospital, more for the sake of his own safety than for the injury itself, and afterwards I had him transferred to E block, where Stoll was already serving his sentence. So it was pure chance that the two men came into contact with each other. Incidentally, on the second, complete list of the prisoner's names, I've had the men in D with Tucker drawn up under a separate heading and those that were around when Tucker fell underlined in red. I didn't know whether you would find it useful to know their names."

"Yes. Thank you," Rudd replied, a little abstractedly. He was deep in thought.

"The time Tucker was in hospital . . ." he began.

"It was only a week," McKinley said. "I didn't think it necessary to find out the names of the men who were in there with him."

"What did Tucker do?" Rudd went on, pursuing his own line of thought. "After all, he couldn't have been lying in bed with a sprained wrist."

"I'll find out," McKinley said, reaching for one of the telephones on his desk. "And I'll get the names of the men who were in the hospital with him. It shouldn't be many."

"Yes, please do," Rudd replied. "It might come in useful."

While McKinley was talking to someone in the prison hospital, Rudd let his mind return to the interview he had had with Tucker at the Blue Boy cafe. Tucker had said he overheard the conversation he had reported to Rudd in a public house off the Strand. Rudd now knew this was a lie. But there could be some element of truth in the story. Long experience of dealing with men who are habitual liars had taught Rudd that, whenever the truth didn't matter to the story they were telling, they tended to include it to avoid confusion and to justify to themselves that part, at least, was accurate and verifiable. It was partly a defence mechanism to protect their self-esteem from the accusation of lying; partly a deliberate trick to confuse any investigation, in the hope that, if some details could be proved to be correct, the whole fabrication might more easily be accepted.

Tucker had said he overheard the two men in the other bar talking behind a screen. The screen might be true. In that case, hospitals had screens that could be wheeled round the bed of a seriously ill patient.

McKinley, who had been listening and taking notes, put down the telephone receiver.

"Tucker spent his time reading magazines, chatting up the other patients if they'd listen to him and pottering about the ward doing odd jobs for the staff. There were, in fact, only a few patients in the hospital at the time. One was an elderly man called Rodgers, an old lag and alcoholic who was, in fact, quietly dying. Another was a stomach ulcer case—Salmon, in for fraud. The third was Lisle, one of our more interesting prisoners, down with a serious attack of influenza."

"Lisle?" said Rudd sharply. The name seemed familiar.

"Yes, Edward Lisle. He's in here with his brother Victor. They got sent down about two years ago on an armed hold-up charge. Altogether they got twelve years, so they've got another ten to serve, five if they get full remission. Usually they're in A block, where we keep men in for the more serious charges. It's not exactly maximum security but they're kept under a stricter surveillance."

"Lisle," said Rudd, repeating the name, trying to place it.

"Bank hold-up in Edmonton. Armed with revolvers. Got caught in the act."

"Yes," said Rudd. "I remember."

It had been on the television news on a day that was short of anything happening internationally, which was probably why it was included. There had been pictures outside of the bank and a short interview with the manager.

"Edward Lisle went down with a bad attack of flu and was moved into the prison hospital. He was quite seriously ill at the time and you might say he's never quite fully recovered. He's a wreck compared to what he was. Of course, it's not only the illness. It's the loss of freedom as well, the sense of futility, especially if a man's in for a long sentence . . ."

Rudd interrupted him to ask, "Could I look round the prison hospital?"

"Of course," McKinley replied, looking only faintly surprised, "if you think it would be useful."

The hospital was a long bare room, looking very much like any public ward built at the period when function and hygiene were considered more important than comfort or beauty, although some effort had been made to cheer the place up with curtains at the windows that did not, however, disguise the heavy bars with which the windows were protected.

It contained eight regulation iron bedsteads, two of which were occupied, each with its own white-painted bedside locker. A table and chairs were placed in the centre of the room, no doubt used by the patients not confined to bed for meals and recreation purposes. The walls, unadorned, were painted cream and the floor had a shine on it like glass. The place smelt of polish, disinfectant and the chemical odours of medicines.

The warder in charge was a pleasant, friendly, middle-aged man, clearly pleased with the opportunity for a chat and the break in the monotony of his day. They talked in a small room off the main ward where, through the glass panels, he could still keep a watch on his patients.

Yes, he remembered Tucker very clearly.

"He wasn't a bad little bloke," he remarked. "Tried to make himself useful, although he was a bit of a nuisance at times—wanting to chat when I was busy. He got on my nerves some days, I'll admit."

"He talked to the other patients?" Rudd hinted gently. He wanted to lead up the subject of Lisle.

"Yes, not that he always got much out of them. There was poor old Rodgers, on his last legs anyway—he's died since. But Tucker used to go and sit by his bed sometimes.

Not that Rodgers had much to say. He'd spent the time when he wasn't in nick quietly drinking himself stupid."

"Salmon?" suggested Rudd.

"Oh, the stomach ulcer. Well, he was a bit out of Tucker's class—a businessman who'd been found fiddling the books. His ulcer made him short-tempered at the best of times. He didn't want much to do with Tucker."

"And Lisle?"

"Lisle was really ill. He'd got flu pretty badly and was running a high temperature for a few days. We'd got him on antibiotics and were keeping a close watch on him in case of complications."

"He had screens round his bed?" Rudd asked.

The warder seemed surprised that Rudd should know of this fact and should take the trouble to mention it.

"Yes, as a matter of fact there were, for the first few days."

"While Tucker was in the ward?"

The man thought for a moment.

"Yes, they would have been. Tucker came in first. Lisle was admitted shortly afterwards. If I remember right, we put screens round him that night and they were left there for the next day at least, if not longer."

Rudd formed the next question carefully, anxious not to arouse the man's suspicions. A prison, like any other closed community, is rife with gossip. He didn't want to run the risk of Lisle finding out that anyone had been asking about him.

"You said Lisle was running a high temperature?"

"That's right. After he was admitted, we were checking it every hour."

"Delirious?" Rudd hinted.

"Yes, he was muttering at one stage. During that first night, he shouted out several times. I wasn't on duty myself but the man who was made a note of it on the medical record."

"Did he shout out anything in particular?"

The warder shrugged.

"Not that I heard. Knowing what patients are like in a delirium, it was probably rubbish. They don't usually talk much sense when they're in that state."

Rudd decided to leave it there. He could, of course, question the warder who had been on night duty at the time but it didn't seem to be necessary. Rudd was certain in his own mind what Lisle had shouted out that night. There were four words. Tucker had already told him what they were.

As he got up to go, he said casually, "I'd rather you didn't mention my visit to anybody. I'm concerned with making a few inquiries about Tucker that I don't want leaked, if I can help it."

It was, he thought, the best way of putting it, leaving the man with the impression that it hadn't been Lisle he was interested in. If he did talk, it was more likely that he would remember the questions he had been asked about Tucker.

Rudd returned to the Governor's office, where McKinley had coffee waiting for him.

"Any luck?" he asked.

"It was useful," admitted Rudd.

He felt a reluctance to discuss the case with McKinley, although he knew anything he told him would be kept confidential. It was more a need to keep what he knew to himself until he had time to think about it in depth.

One thing was certain: he now knew the circumstances under which Tucker had overheard those four words. He also knew the identity of the man who had spoken them and this confirmed the impression he had had during the interview with Tucker at the Blue Boy cafe that Tucker himself knew who the man was. Of course he did. He must have been aware that the delirious man behind the screen in the prison hospital was Edward Lisle, in for armed robbery.

All along Rudd had had the impression that it concerned something big. Well, armed robbery would fit into that category. Certainly, the law considered it a serious crime. Lisle and his brother had been kept under special surveillance in A block.

He still didn't know where the murder of Melanie Thorpe fitted into all this. But, at least, he was a step further along the road to finding a solution, although he would need to know more about Edward Lisle first.

He remembered Detective Chief Inspector Reggie Monk of Scotland Yard's C.I.D. Rudd had once been involved in a case in which he had liaised with Monk and the two men had got on well together. They had struck up a friendship that they still maintained, meeting occasionally for a drink.

McKinley could no doubt tell Rudd something of Lisle, but the chances were Monk would be better informed about his criminal activities. He had access to the files at the Yard.

Rudd decided to telephone Monk at home that evening, making it an unofficial inquiry at this stage. He didn't want to put the whole ponderous machinery of the law into operation over four words spoken by a man in a delirium.

Having taken leave of McKinley, Rudd left Parkgate, stopping off at a public library on the outskirts of London where, in the hushed gloom of the reference section, he looked up the word "transit" in one of the big dictionaries. Reading quickly down the lines of tiny print, he skipped over the more obvious meanings—"conveyance," "a line of passage," "a route." And then his finger stopped further down the page at an unfamiliar expression. "Transit point" he read. "A navigational aid." The letters *"naut.,"* which he took to be an abbreviation for "nautical," were enclosed in brackets after the words.

Deep in thought, he copied it down, then closed the dictionary and replaced it on the shelf and left.

Boyce was in the office, still gloomily going through the witnesses' statements from the Thorpe file when Rudd returned. A sheet of paper at his side already contained more than fifty names and addresses. He looked up eagerly when Rudd entered, hoping for a diversion, and Rudd, who hadn't yet had any lunch, sent out for tea and sandwiches from the canteen.

While they were eating them, Rudd briefly described the day's events and what he had discovered at Parkgate prison. The name Lisle, however, meant nothing to Boyce. He couldn't remember the case at all.

"Well, anyway, I'm going to get in touch with Monk this evening and fix a meeting. He ought to be able to tell us something about him."

"And that's where you reckon Tucker overheard that conversation—in the prison hospital?"

"I'm certain in my own mind," Rudd replied.

"You could always round up Tucker and ask him," Boyce pointed out.

"Not yet," said Rudd. "Maybe later. But I don't want to tip off either Stoll or Tucker that I know what case it is that's involved. By the way, I forgot to mention it the other day that Tucker spoke of another word he'd overheard. 'Transit.' "

"Transit?"

"I stopped on the way back and looked it up in a dictionary. Among the various meanings listed, there was one that could be significant."

Taking the scrap of paper out of his pocket, he read out, " 'Transit point: a navigational aid.' It's a nautical term, according to the dictionary."

"Don't get it," mumbled Boyce, through a mouthful of sandwich.

"Boats," said Rudd. "Merestead's on the coast and there's several yachting centres nearby. See if you can lay your hands on a large-scale map of the area. Meanwhile, there's one other point I want to check on; the report from forensic on Melanie Thorpe's clothing."

"I've already been through that," Boyce said quickly, as if on the defensive. "There was nothing in it of use that I could see."

It seemed to Rudd a good moment to get the Sergeant out of the office while he went over the report himself. Boyce, thick-skinned and unimaginative in some ways, had his raw spots and one of them was any suggestion that he hadn't been thorough in his work.

"Nip downstairs and get that map, will you?" Rudd asked.

While Boyce was away, Rudd read rapidly through the typewritten pages. He knew what he was looking for was a mere detail, something that seemed relatively trivial. He found it at last towards the bottom of the page.

"The outer clothing, particularly the legs of the trousers, had white hairs, probably a dog's, clinging to them."

Boyce returned at this moment and Rudd barely had time to replace the report in the file before he entered. There was certainly no opportunity to consider the detail he had just read.

"Here we are, then," Boyce announced, opening the map out across the desk top. They both bent over it.

"Merestead," said Rudd, finding it on the coast. He ran his finger south along the deeply indented line that followed in tiny scale the intricacies of the creeks and inlets that he had seen something of himself two days before. "And here's Tolquay. That's a sailing centre, isn't it, Tom?"

Boyce shrugged.

"I think so. I've never been keen on boats myself."

Rudd ran his finger further on.

"Or there's West Turnham, a few miles on up the coast."

He made a quick calculation of distances from the scale of the map. Tolquay was about five miles from Merestead if one took a direct route, probably much further if one went by road or even approached it by water. The map did not show the channels; he'd need a chart for that. But, from the little he knew about the coast-line and navigation, he doubted if it would be a simple matter of sailing from one point to another.

Returning to Merestead, he followed with the point of a pencil the route he had gone over the previous Saturday, tracing the windings of the road. Just beyond Hadley Corner, he made a tiny mark, to indicate the place where Melanie Thorpe's body had been found. Then the pencil moved on again, back to Wiston.

Boyce watched him.

"Did you find out anything useful on that trip?" he asked.

"Not much," admitted Rudd. "Nothing factual, anyway. Just a few impressions."

He left it there, not wishing at that stage to discuss it with the Sergeant. His own ideas were still too vague.

"Did Stoll follow you?"

"No, Miller drew him off, as we'd hoped. And today, I managed to give him the slip in the traffic. He's back on the job, though. I noticed him parked in the cul-de-sac when I got back from Parkgate."

"Persistent devil, isn't he?" said Boyce. He added, following an earlier train of thought of his own, "We know Stoll and Tucker probably met up in Parkgate, but I wonder what made Tucker tell Stoll what he'd overheard?"

"Knowing Tucker, probably no more than a desire to chat to somebody," Rudd replied with an abstracted air. His thoughts were elsewhere.

Boyce, realising this, made the most of the opportunity. "I'll push off, then, if there's nothing else?" he suggested, and as Rudd only grunted in reply, he took it as assent and, putting on his overcoat, made for the door.

In the door-way he paused to add, "By the way, the man who called at the newspaper office was Stoll. Hillmore, the man in charge of their files, recognised the touched-up photograph."

He went quickly, before Rudd had time to call him back.

Rudd was almost relieved to see him go. Ideas were beginning to stir and he needed peace and quiet to think them out. Standing hump-shouldered at the window, gazing out but hardly aware of the view, he let his mind drift.

Dog's hairs. It was a tiny detail and one that he ought to have remembered. After all, he himself had fended off the dog when it came sidling up to him when he called at the house-boat, knowing that it had shed its hairs all over the matting and chairs in Thorpe's cottage. But was it relevant? Wouldn't it be inevitable that Melanie would have got them on her clothing?

He thought of the dog, as he had scrambled ashore from Thorpe's boat, looking up at him in anticipation and then lying down again when it realised it was only the Inspector.

Rudd knew what the dog had been expecting with such subdued hope: the walk into the village along the sea-wall to the Anchor with Thorpe. He saw again the two figures making their way home, silhouetted against the wide sky; Thorpe in front, the dog padding along a little distance behind.

It was a question of habit. Thorpe always went to the Anchor at lunch-time and the dog knew it. But, on the last day his daughter visited him, he had broken with this custom; no doubt feeling it would be unkind to leave her alone when she had come all that way to see him. After all, Thorpe wasn't entirely without sensibilities and his own code of conduct.

Plastic containers. His mind kept coming back to them. He saw them lying about on the floor; some lined up against the wall. And then he made the connection.

Of course! What they were linked with in his mind was the collection of empty beer bottles standing in the fireplace of the cottage. He had seen them when he called on Thorpe on the Monday, the day his daughter's body had been found. Thorpe hadn't yet got round to returning them.

Rudd was certain now what Thorpe had done that Sunday afternoon. Although not wishing to go to the pub, he hadn't been able to completely forgo his habit of lunch-time drinking. So, instead of going out to the Anchor, he had brought the beer to the house.

Rudd guessed what had happened after that. He recalled the man's uneasiness, the eagerness with which he had hurried the conversation along with the remark "And then she got tea," as if he had been anxious not to discuss in too much detail what had happened earlier in the afternoon. The answer was, Thorpe had been asleep or too hazy with drink to remember very clearly what Melanie had been doing, and had been ashamed to admit it.

The odd remark "I remember she come through to sweep the floor" now made sense. It was probably the only thing Thorpe did remember with any clarity of the hours following the midday meal.

Thorpe had been asleep and Melanie had supposedly been busy about the house. This was the story that Thorpe had told. But Thorpe's version could no longer be relied on. She had washed the floor and laundered some shirts. He had the neighbour's evidence to prove that. But was that enough to keep her occupied while her father slept? It was clear now that they hadn't talked and clear, too, that the supposition he had made that she had remained all day with her father in the cottage was no longer supportable.

He came back to the dog's hairs found on her clothing; mostly, as the report had said, on the front of the trousers she was wearing. The dog could have jumped up to greet her when she first arrived, of course. It was the family pet, after all, and she was fond of animals. Allowing for this, what would have been more natural than for her to take the dog for a walk while her father slept in the living-room?

And if that was so, as Rudd now began to think it might be, it therefore followed that she could have met someone on that walk who later offered her a lift at the bus stop and then killed her.

He looked at his watch. It was too late to return to Merestead and requestion Thorpe. That would have to wait for another day.

Meanwhile, he had a further line of investigation that he could start to follow up straightaway: Edward Lisle.

"Eddy Lisle?" said Monk when Rudd phoned him at home later that evening. "Good God! Is it an official inquiry?"

"No," said Rudd guardedly. "Just a chat at this stage. Could we meet fairly soon?"

"At the Yard?"

"I'd prefer somewhere less formal," Rudd replied.

Monk laughed.

"I get the message. Well, I could arrange to be free tomorrow lunch-time, say around twelve-thirty. If you happened to drop in at Rose Tavern, just off Cornhill, we could chat over a meal. How does that suit you?"

"Twelve-thirty it is," said Rudd and rang off.

8

The Rose Tavern was a discreetly lit, dark-panelled eating house, consisting of one long room with separate dining compartments along both sides, that reminded Rudd of comfortable and elegant loose boxes.

Monk was already there, craning his head round the panelling of one of the boxes, flapping a napkin to attract Rudd's attention. Rudd walked down the length of the room, over dark red carpeting that felt like sponge underfoot, and slid into his place on the padded leather bench opposite the Chief Inspector.

Rudd was feeling particularly pleased with life. Not only was he seeing Monk again, whose company he enjoyed, and in a setting that none of his local towns had to offer, but he had successfully ditched Stoll at Liverpool Street station, having deliberately lured the man that far on the train in a perverse desire to play the man along until the last possible minute and then had turned it neatly, getting onto an underground train bound for the Bank just as the doors were closing, leaving Stoll, seconds too late, on the platform.

"Nice," said Rudd appreciatively, looking about him.

"I thought you'd like it," Monk replied. "That's why I suggested it. The food's good, so's the beer. And we can talk without being disturbed." He looked at Rudd and laughed.

"God! You look more like a farmer every time I see you."

"Protective colouring," Rudd replied equably. "I like to feel I melt into the landscape."

He didn't comment, as he might have done, that Monk

had his own protective colouring that suited his own background. Monk was a Londoner and proud of it, carrying with him an air of chirpy self-sufficiency that Rudd had noticed in other Cockneys, barrow-boys, market-porters, taxi-drivers; an ability to take life as it came and, if possible, give it back as good as it gave. He was a small-featured, thin-cheeked man, with quick brown eyes that were constantly on the move, looking things over, noticing everything, bright with laughter one second, hard and watchful the next.

A waiter came over with the menu.

"The steak and mushroom pie's good," Monk advised.

It was, too; the top layer of pastry light and flaky, the bottom moist and succulent with gravy and meat juices.

"Eddy Lisle," said Monk, picking up the conversation of the evening before. "Any particular reason why you're interested?"

"It's an old case," Rudd replied as if casually. He was not anxious at this stage to give much away, even to Monk. "His name drifted my way. He probably hasn't anything to do with it but it got me intrigued and I'd like to follow it up."

Monk gave him a bright, thoughtful look over a forkful of steak and mushroom pie.

"Unofficially?"

"At this stage, yes."

Monk was silent for a moment. Then he seemed to make up his mind. Leaning forward across the table, he began to speak in a low, rapid voice.

"Eddy Lisle. One of the Lisle brothers. There's four of them. Frank, Eddy, Vic and Bunny. East End family. Father used to run a clothing stall in Petticoat Lane. No form, but when the Yard started looking into the family background, they discovered old man Lisle was probably a bit bent. There was talk of war-time black-market clothing coupons; stuff disappearing from bombed warehouses, that sort of thing. It's neither here nor there now; old Lisle's dead anyway, but it fills in a bit of family history. The mother's still alive. Lives in a nice, comfortable modern flat in Hoxton paid for by her ever-loving sons. And I'm not being sarcastic. They are one of those tight-knit East End families that closes ranks on the first sign of trouble from the outside world.

"Frank's the eldest. He started off by helping his father run the market stall. Then he gradually went up in the world. He went into the wholesale side of the clothing business and runs a chain of cheap boutiques round White-chapel and Stepney. I met him once. He's a good-looking well-dressed man in his mid-forties. Married with a couple of kids. Very respectable. Drives a Rover and wears a camel-hair overcoat. You know the type? But still showing his origins, if you know where to look for them.

"There was a gap of four years before the next Lisle brother, Eddy, was born. It's important to remember the gap. It put Frank in the position of the elder brother and head of the family when his father died. After Eddy came Vic, only eleven months later, so they grew up together, more like twins, and have always been very close. I haven't met either of them so I can't tell you much except they went into business together with money loaned to them by big brother Frank; a small paint-spray and welding shop in Stepney which made some profit although not a lot. They shared the flat over the business. Vic had never married. Eddy had been once, but it hadn't worked out and he'd been divorced. There were no children. They'd kept their street trading licence and, when business was slack at the work-shop, they'd go round the local markets selling clothing that Frank supplied.

"There was another gap of five years before the last brother, James, usually called 'Bunny,' was born. So while Frank was very much the elder brother, Bunny was the younger, with the sort of privileges that younger sons often get. He went to the grammar school for example and later took up a job away from the family surroundings. The other Lisle brothers were reluctant to talk much about Bunny and we got the impression that he was the white sheep of the family who'd done the unforgivable thing by becoming middle-class and turning his back on his East End origins. I'll come back to him later.

"So, we have the four Lisle brothers, with Frank the dominant one, who's made it big-time in the East End business world, Vic and Eddy, who still seem under Frank's influence and patronage to some extent, and Bunny, who seems to have moved right out of the family picture. You're with me?"

"Yes," said Rudd. "I'm with you."

"And no form," said Monk. "The police had nothing on them, apart from an occasional parking ticket and one fine for speeding on Eddy."

He paused, as if that part of the narrative were finished, beginning again after a few seconds' pause.

"About ten years ago there were a series of armed hold-ups on small, good-class jewellers on the outskirts of London. They all followed the same pattern. A well-dressed, well-built man would come into the shop, leaving his chauffeur-driven car parked nearby, and ask to see some jewellery for a tenth-wedding anniversary present for his wife. He was shown some of the more expensive pieces and while he was looking them over, trying to make up his mind, a uniformed police motor-cyclist, dressed in goggles and helmet, came in to ask whose car it was parked outside as it was causing an obstruction. The manager's attention was naturally diverted from the customer. The next thing he knew, both men had produced guns, the well-dressed man told him to hand over the jewellery and they had made a quick get-away in the car, which was later found abandoned.

"There were six of these raids altogether and the gang netted about £75,000 worth of jewels from them. The police did the obvious things; issued descriptions for a start, not that they were much use. None of the witnesses got a good look at the police motor-cyclist because of the helmet and goggles, and few passers-by bothered to take a second look at the chauffeur, except to notice he was in uniform and wearing a peaked cap. As for the third man, the one who posed as the customer, they got so many different descriptions of him that it was obvious that he was disguised; and cleverly disguised, too. When we tried making up Identi-kit pictures, the witnesses disagreed even about the shape of his nose and the angle of the eyebrows.

"There were no finger-prints either. The motor-cyclist wore gauntlets, the customer wore gloves, which he only removed to examine the jewellery when it was laid out for his inspection on a velvet or felt cloth on top of the counter and he was careful to put them on again so he left nothing in the way of prints either on the counter or the door.

"But we did have something to go on. There were three of them. Of the two who came into the shop, the motor-cyclist was slightly built, the other man was tall and broad-shouldered. Now, you can disguise height and build up to a point. You can make a short man look taller or a thin man look fatter, but you can't make a tall, broad-shouldered man look any different from the point of view of his physique.

"Voices, too, can be disguised, we've learned to our cost. The man who posed as the customer spoke with a faint London accent, the motor-cyclist with a Midlands one. This was to prove a red-herring, as we found out afterwards that Vic had worked for a few months on a building site in Birmingham and could have picked up the lingo.

"The other positive fact we had to go on was that, as a gang, they were very well-organised. The shops they raided were carefully chosen. As I said, they were all good-class jewellers, the sort that was likely to carry the more expensive items, and they were all in quiet shopping areas where traffic wasn't too heavy, so parking the car and getting away afterwards wouldn't be too difficult. The cars, incidentally, were all stolen, with false number plates. They also chose a day when the towns were less crowded and there'd be few passers-by to witness the raids.

"The other fact that emerged was that as far as the underworld was concerned they were unknown. All our usual contacts knew nothing about them. They were as puzzled as we were. We kept a watch on the usual fences, those that dealt in stolen jewellery, but none of it surfaced. And it still hasn't. We also kept a watch on the West End clubs, looking for anyone who was in the money and spending freely. The usual crook, however clever he is, lacks one important quality: a long-term view of life. He'll do a bank, say, and then spend the proceeds quite quickly afterwards. If we don't spot him ourselves chucking the loot about the West End, then someone else will and the word gets passed on to us—'So and so's in funds.' But these men didn't fall into that trap. Whatever happened to the jewellery, it wasn't turned into cash for spending.

"There was a gap of about two years before the next series of armed raids began, this time on banks. Like the hold-ups on the jewellers, they followed a pattern. A security van, or what looked like one, would draw up outside the bank and the two men, dressed in the firm's uniforms, complete with goggles and helmets, would come in and one of them would speak to a clerk. 'It was a special consignment of cash,' he'd say. The next instant, both men had produced guns and while one of them herded any customers who might be in the bank at the time up to one end away from the door, the other ordered the clerks to hand over the money. The two men then did a quick get-away in the van, which was later found abandoned.

"In five raids, it was reckoned they made a cool £100,000, all in Bank of England notes. It didn't take long to establish a link with the earlier hold-ups. Again, three men were involved, two who were armed and carried out the robberies, one who drove the get-away van. Although the actual sites chosen were different, banks this time, not shops, there was a similarity in style, particularly in the use of uniforms. Apart from the fact that any uniform in itself is a good disguise—who notices what a postman or a milkman looks like if you pass him in the street?—the goggles and helmets worn by the police motor-cyclist and the security guards were, in themselves, an excellent means of covering up the face and making identification difficult, even by those witnesses actually involved in the hold-ups.

"Again, as in the robberies on the jewellers, there were no prints; both men wore gloves. But all the witnesses agreed that one man was tall and well-built, the other slighter and thinner. The vans they used gave us a few useful leads, too. They were ordinary commercial vehicles, stolen, of course, but done up to look like security vans; painted black with the right markings, and grilles on the windows; not a really professional job, but good enough to fool most people.

"So we deduced from this that the gang had access to welding and spraying equipment. As most of the cars had been stolen in the areas on the east side of London and the robberies had tended to take place in the same general direction, the south-eastern counties, we started making inquiries at all the garages and work-shops on that side of London, working outwards. It took months, involved hundreds of men and got us nowhere. Funnily enough, Vic and Eddy's work-shop was one of those looked over but it was written off as being too small. There was only a tiny yard at the back, certainly not large enough to have kept a stolen van in without someone noticing. The uniforms were another lead we tried following up and we made inquiries at wholesalers, clothing manufacturers, costume-hire firms, but nothing came of that either. According to the witnesses that got a good look at them, they could have been home-made, or at least adapted from trousers and jackets that you can buy almost anywhere. Someone, with a bit of tailoring skill, could easily have altered them. As it turned out later, Frank Lisle could have done them. He'd picked up enough knowledge of the clothing manufacturing business over the years to make a reasonable enough job of the alterations.

"Our best bet was the underworld itself. But, like the raids on the jewellers, no-one knew anything. It wasn't honour among thieves either. There's always someone willing to grass, out of malice or envy, or personal revenge, or to keep in with the law. The banks had offered rewards as well but even that didn't draw any information. There wasn't a whisper. And, again, there was no sign of anyone spending the loot, although we raided some clubs and pulled in a few villains who seemed a bit flush for funds, they weren't the ones we were looking for.

"It was at this stage of going round the clubs that I got personally involved in the inquiries. The case intrigued me, particularly from the psychological angle. The raids were so bloody cheeky. The use of the uniforms interested me as well. These men were deliberately identifying themselves with the law. If a police motor-cyclist walks into a shop or a couple of security guards into a bank, the average person around at the time assumes they're good guys, on the side of law and order. The shock and surprise when they pull out guns is therefore all the more shattering. The shop assistants and bank clerks all experienced this moment of total bewilderment in which they admitted they couldn't think of anything to do. They just stood there, totally at a loss. It gave the criminals an enormous psychological advantage. You get my point?"

Rudd nodded.

"It got up my nose for that reason," Monk went on. "They were cool, clever and well-organised. The choice of banks they raided was revealing, too. They were local branches, in quiet areas, unlikely to have many customers in them at any one time and with few passers-by, but close enough to industrial or commercial centres to carry a large amount of ready cash.

"The money, by the way, vanished, like the jewellery, without trace and never reappeared.

"After this, there was a quiet spell for about a year. Then came a couple of hold-ups of a different nature, although we soon realised the same men were involved. One was on a diamond merchant in Hatton Garden. The owner was in the habit of dining alone on a Friday evening at his club as a quiet end to the week. A message was brought to him one Friday by the porter, who said there was a policeman outside asking to see him. The man went into the entrance hall where a police motorcyclist was waiting to tell him that his wife had been involved in an accident and was in hospital seriously injured. A police car was standing at the kerb, ready to rush him to her bed-side. What would you do in the circumstances? I know I'd've done the same as he did—go straight out of the club to the waiting car. Once inside the car, though, he realised it was a trick. The two men in it weren't police at all, although they were in uniform. One was driving. One sat in the back with him, and pulled a gun on him as soon as he sat down. He was told nothing would happen to him if he did exactly as he was told.

"He was driven to his office, where he was forced to open the safe and hand over its contents, £150,000 worth of diamonds. There was a security man in the building but he suspected nothing. In fact, the police motor-cyclist kept him busy in the corridor outside, chatting him up, explaining that something had gone wrong with the alarm system that was connected with the local police station and they'd come round to check it out. The security man believed him. After all, these men were police. The diamond merchant had let them in with his own keys. It all seemed perfectly acceptable. Presently the diamond merchant came out, accompanied by the policeman, and they all drove off in the police car, the motor-cyclist following behind on his bike. The man was later dumped at the roadside on the outskirts of London and by the time he'd got to a phone, the villains must have been miles away.

"Notice the similarity to the previous raids? The use of uniforms; the identification with the law; the cool, bloody cheek of it? Three men were again involved. One remained in the car, as driver, which was done up to look like an official vehicle, even to the blue light on the roof; one who acted the part of the police motor-cyclist, so neither the diamond merchant nor the security man got a good look at his face and could say very little about his appearance except he was slightly built compared to the third man, passing himself off as a sergeant, who went with the merchant into the office. We had a better description of him, especially from the merchant but, as he was obviously disguised, the details, thick eyebrows, reddish hair and moustache, weren't much use. He was described by both men, however, as being tall and well-built.

"The second raid was on a bullion merchant in the city, and while the details were different, there were enough similarities to tie it in with the other robberies. This time it happened in the day-time, during working hours. The bullion dealer got a telephone call in his office. The man on the other end told him that he was holding his wife at gunpoint in his home in Surrey but no harm would come to her if he followed instructions. Two security guards would be calling shortly at his office. He was to hand over to them all the bullion in his strong room and not raise the alarm for an hour afterwards, otherwise his wife would be for it. She was put on the line and confirmed the story—a man was standing over her with a gun. She sounded very frightened. The husband assured her he would do as he had been told. Five minutes later, when two security men in uniform walked into his office, he unlocked the strong room and watched while they cleared it of £250,000 of gold, silver and platinum in bars and coins. They made several trips out to their van. The rest of the staff suspected nothing. They knew a big deal was in the offing and they thought the arrangements for the transfer of the bullion had been brought forward. After all, they were proper security men, wearing the right uniforms and driving an official vehicle and the merchant had let them in and opened up the strong room for them. An hour later, as instructed, he raised the alarm. He'd already tried phoning his home, but the line was dead. The wife was found, bound and gagged but otherwise unharmed. She'd been held up by a man wearing a stocking mask and carrying a gun and, apart from the fact that he seemed youngish and was well-spoken, she could tell us nothing of his appearance. He'd left about half an hour after the raid had taken place, ripping out the phone before he went, so all of them had an hour's start on the police.

"This last raid had one interesting variation: four men were involved this time. Apart from this, the pattern was basically the same—the uniforms, the official-looking vehicle, the coolness and organisation behind it. The last hold-up had been very carefully timed, too. But the robberies on the two dealers suggested something else more significant. Both of them were putting through big deals in the next few days and were carrying extra-large stocks of diamonds and bullion; more than they usually held. It suggested that the gang had some inside information. They also knew that the diamond merchant had a house in Surrey, isolated, with no immediate neighbours who would notice anything suspicious and that the bullion dealer was in the habit of dining alone in his club on a Friday evening. We checked it out but it didn't seem to lead anywhere much at the time, although it was later to prove an interesting link with the Lisle brothers.

"The loot disappeared as before and the underworld still knew nothing, so we were no further forward in identifying the criminals, although, by this time, we had enough on paper, statements by witnesses and so on, to fill a complete filing cabinet at the Yard."

"So you had nothing at this stage to connect the raids with the Lisle brothers?" Rudd asked.

"Not a whisper," Monk replied. "The Lisle brothers were going quietly about their lives, as they had always done. As I told you, they had no form. They weren't even on a list of suspects. As far as the police were concerned, they no more existed than do millions of other people who pay their taxes and live ordinary, honest, law-abiding lives. With hindsight, I can see Frank Lisle must have kept a very tight rein on Vic and Eddy. I'm certain he was the brains behind the organisation and, as the elder brother, he saw to it that they didn't spend more than usual. There were no sudden purchases of expensive cars or clothes to make the neighbours sit up and take notice. The three of them just went on as they'd always done, Frank running his wholesale business, Vic and Eddy their little back-street work-shop, with occasional trips out of London to run a clothing stall in some market or other, and Bunny—well, as I said before, I'll come back to him later.

"It could have gone on like this for years, if they hadn't had a stroke of bad luck. About eighteen months after the raid on the bullion dealer, another bank-raid took place. It followed the same pattern as before: a security van was parked outside, two men in uniform entered the building. Only this time something went badly wrong. There was a genuine Securicor visit scheduled to call at the bank shortly afterwards. The two real officials saw the bogus van, realized something was up and radioed an alarm before entering the building. The driver panicked and drove off, leaving the other two villains inside, where they were held by the two guards until the police arrived. Luckily, they were taken by surprise and no shoot-up took place. They were arrested by the police and taken to the local station where they admitted their identity. They were Vic and Eddy Lisle. Although they refused to name the driver of the van, we suspected it was Frank Lisle but nothing could be proved against him. His wife said he was home in bed with gastric flu and, as he'd gone to the trouble to call in a doctor the day before who'd examined him and was prepared to swear he seemed genuinely ill, we had to let the case against him drop for lack of evidence.

"But at least we had Vic and Eddy in the bag and, we were convinced in our minds, two of the men involved in the previous robberies. But brother Frank got a sharp lawyer to defend them who pleaded that Vic and Eddy had read about the robberies in the newspapers at the time and had used them, so to speak, as a paper pattern for their own hold-up. It worked, too. We put them up for identity parades and had every person remotely connected as witnesses with the other robberies to take a look at them. A few picked them out but not enough to convince the jury. As their lawyer pointed out, very cleverly, there'd been a recent case of wrongful arrest following an identity parade, so the jury gave them the benefit of the doubt and they were found guilty on the one count and were given twelve years for that crime only.

"Now, I'm perfectly convinced that Frank Lisle was as deeply involved as his two brothers. I think he posed as the customer in that first series of raids on the jewellers. He has that prosperous air about him that would make him right for the part. Vic, the more slightly built of the brothers, was the motor-cyclist and Eddy acted as chauffeur. But in the later hold-ups, those on the banks and the two robberies in the City, it's my belief that they swapped roles round a bit and Frank took over the job of driver, leaving Vic and Eddy to do the actual raids. But after a lapse of time, the scent gets a bit cold.

"We did, however, unearth one interesting fact. If you remember, I told you we'd made intensive inquiries at the time of the bank raids into any garage or work-shop that could have done up the stolen vans to look like security vehicles and Vic and Eddy's place was visited but was written off as being too small? Well, we hunted about and came up with a bit of evidence about a man calling himself Morrison and looking a bit like Frank Lisle who'd rented a small warehouse and yard not far away from Vic and Eddy's place. The man who'd rented it out couldn't make a positive i.d. He said it was a long time ago and he had a bad memory for faces. He'd been paid in cash, so no cheque had changed hands and my guess is he hadn't declared it for taxation and, not wanting to get involved, he wasn't anxious to let on he knew very much. But I think it was in that rented warehouse that Vic and Eddy did the alterations on the stolen vehicles. They had the equipment, the spray guns and the welding gear. It was simply a matter of transporting it over there where there was no danger they'd be seen at work on them."

"Morrison?" asked Rudd. "You said that was the name Frank Lisle used?"

Monk gave him a quick, searching look.

"Yes. Does it mean anything to you?"

"No," replied Rudd. "I've never heard of it."

But it was a useful name to remember. He knew that criminals tend to use the same alias time and time again.

"Sorry," he added. "Go on."

Monk looked a bit put out. By interrupting him, Rudd had made him lose the thread of his story.

"Where was I? Oh, yes. There was one other fact that tended to point to Vic and Eddy at least being involved in the other hold-ups. Most of them had taken place in towns or districts where there were street markets. We know Vic and Eddy were in the habit of running a clothing stall when business at the work-shop was slack. In fact, the records showed that they'd been to all those markets, which would have given them the opportunity to get to know where likely banks and jewellers were, what traffic conditions were like and the quickest route out of the place.

"The other brother I haven't said very much about so far is the youngest, Bunny Lisle. He's the one who had the grammar school education and seemed to have moved away from his old family connections. When they were interviewed, the other three put up quite a convincing show of not knowing much about him. In fact, he'd been working for the past few years in a stockbroker's office in the City and I'm convinced it was through Bunny that they got their inside information about the diamond and bullion dealers. He was evidently a personable young man. I say 'evidently' because by the time we got round to making full inquiries about him, he'd already left the country, no-one seemed to know where. The other brothers said they knew nothing about him; in fact, hadn't seen him for years. I'll admit it took us a while to make the connection between Bunny Lisle, son of an East End street trader, and James Lisle, popular young man about town, with a host of friends among the clerks and junior accountants in the other City offices. We were a bit slow off the mark there. But one of Bunny's hobbies was amateur dramatics. He was the leading light in a group in Richmond and, guess what? He'd done a course in stage make-up run by a drama school in the evenings. I think that's how Frank and the others, when they weren't covered up with goggles and helmets, were so well-disguised that it made identification impossible.

"Anyway, I'm sure in my own mind that Bunny was the fourth man on the raid on the bullion dealer, the one who held up the man's wife at gun-point. And I think he skipped the country because there were too many positive trails that led to him; the City background in general; the fact that he was friendly with a clerk at both the bullion dealer's and the diamond merchant's, or on lunch-time drinking terms with them; that he'd done a course in stage make-up; and, finally, on the day of the robbery he'd been away from the office; sick, so he said.

"But there was something else more important behind

his removal. We were fooled for a time into thinking that
Bunny had broken with his family. If my thinking's correct, he'd been sent ahead."

"Sent ahead?" Rudd asked.

"Look at it this way," Monk replied. "We never recovered any of the loot they stole. Somewhere there's nearly
three quarters of a million pounds' worth of jewellery, cash
and bullion stashed away. My guess is it's their equivalent
of a sockful of money under the mattress. One day, not yet,
because old Mrs. Lisle's still alive and kicking down in
Hoxton, and the Lisle brothers are nothing if not loyal to
their old ma; but one day they were planning to do a quiet
flit to some tax-haven where three quarters of a million
pounds' worth of investment could have set them up very
nicely for the rest of their lives. As far as they were concerned, it could have looked legitimate. Frank Lisle sells
out and retires early, joined by Vic and Eddy, while Bunny
had already gone ahead of them to prepare the ground. He
may already be establishing himself as a well-to-do English
ex-patriate, investing some of the takings. I don't know.
Interpol hasn't been able to trace him. And it's my guess,
too, that if we hadn't caught Vic and Eddy when we did,
they might have gone on for several more years, doing a
raid here and there, adding to the family stocking. As it is,
with Vic and Eddy inside, their plans will have to be post-
poned for a few years. They're likely to get parole after five
to six years, so maybe they planned their flit for then."

He stopped and looked at Rudd, his brown eyes watchful.

"That's the story so far. We're waiting for the next in-
stallment. And, for God's sake man, if you know anything
of importance, hand it over to the Yard. Apart from the
three quarters of a million quid'sworth of loot that's never
been recovered, there were thousands of man hours in-
vested in the Lisle case, not to mention the reputation of
some very high-ranking officers, the sort of blokes you and
I touch our caps to. As far as they're concerned the case
hasn't been closed. Vic and Eddy Lisle got sent down for
twelve years on the one charge. There's thirteen others
waiting to be pinned on them, so, otherwise you could finish up with your head on the chopping-block. They won't
like it if some local inspector wades in on his own and
makes a balls-up of it."

Rudd arranged his knife and fork neatly side by side on his empty plate and looked bland.

"Thanks for the warning. But, at the moment, all I'm doing is making a few inquiries into a case of my own that's never been closed and one that couldn't possibly interest the Yard."

"And all I'm doing," Monk interposed, "is having an unofficial chat with a colleague over lunch about an interesting set of villains on a swap-shop basis. Right?"

"Right," Rudd agreed.

He added, later, as they parted company outside on the pavement:

"I might be in touch sometime; officially, that is."

Monk acknowledged this with a quick wave of his hand an then was off, moving nimbly through the city crowds, hardly brushing against the other pedestrians as he went.

9

Stoll picked him up again as he returned to Liverpool Street station and it gave Rudd a certain satisfaction to think that the man had been forced to hang about there for nearly two hours.

He let him tail him back to headquarters. After all, what was the harm in that? But, the following day, he decided he must lose him again and this time for good. The inquiries he now had to follow up were too important to allow Stoll so much as a sniff at them.

It was accomplished the next morning, as before, with Miller's help: Miller driving off in Rudd's car while Rudd, who had already reserved a room by telephone at the White Hart hotel at Boxleigh, left later in Miller's car, carrying an overnight bag. For the next couple of days he would be free of Stoll. Miller had been given instructions to abandon the disguise once he arrived at headquarters and to leave Rudd's car standing in the car-park. Stoll would, of course, realise that something was up but that would have to be risked.

Having booked into the hotel, Rudd drove from Boxleigh to Merestead, leaving the car in the village centre and walking down the lane to Thorpe's old cottage.

If his supposition was correct, that Thorpe had spent at least part of that Sunday afternoon asleep and the worse for drink, Melanie could have taken the dog for a walk. He stood at the gate of the derelict house, thinking. Which way had she gone? She hadn't been seen in the village and, although this was mere negative evidence and proved very little, he was inclined to accept the possibility that, if she had walked that way, someone might have seen her.

The only other direction she could have taken was down the lane, away from the village. Thorpe's cottage was the last house. The chances of any witnesses seeing her walking the dog if she went that way were less likely.

He started off in that direction, down the lane and away from the village. Soon after he had left the cottage, the lane narrowed down to a mere track, running between high hedges, at the end of which was a stile. Beyond lay a field across which a faint footpath ran and beyond that the high, grassy slope of the sea-wall, cutting off any further view.

Climbing the stile, Rudd set off across the field, following the track and, scrambling up the slope of the dyke, came to the path that ran along its top. Here the view widened out to the marshes and the sea, a view very similar to the one he had seen on the other side of the village when he had visited Thorpe's house-boat. From the dyke top he could pick out the roof-tops of the houses, clustered together among the trees, and the tower of the church, poking above them. He turned right, walking along the top of the dyke, away from the village, following the broad creek running alongside it, which the sea-wall was designed to hold back from the pasture land on its further side.

He had already worked out an estimate of the time she could have spent on the walk. Allowing for the house-hold chores she had done during the afternoon, it probably couldn't have been much more than an hour, half an hour there, half an hour back; although it was only an approximate time-table.

When the half-hour was up, he stopped and looked about him. The view hadn't substantially changed. The village was further off, the roof-tops now almost indistinguishable among the surrounding trees. The fields still lay to his right, grazing land occupied by a herd of cows moving peacefully across them. To his left, the creek still lapped the bottom of the sea-wall. That hadn't changed much either, except it had broadened out and was now about twelve feet wide. The tide was full and the water was at its highest point.

If she had gone for a walk and if she had come along this path and if she had met someone on that walk, there were only three ways in which that person could have arrived: by foot, across the fields or along the dyke path, or by water along the creek itself. If. If. If.

Rudd looked down thoughtfully at the creek. It still wasn't all that wide but it might be navigable. He remembered the word "transit"—a navigational aid as the dictionary had defined it.

But why should anyone want to bring a boat up that particular channel? There was nothing that could suggest any reason; no boat-house; no landing-stage; just the saltings stretching away to one side and on the other the sheer bank of the sea-wall. There wasn't so much as a post or a stake to indicate a mooring place.

He stared down at it for some time and then, defeated, turned back towards the village, following the way he had come, past Thorpe's old cottage and the Anchor, to the other side of the marshes, where he climbed the wooden steps at the fore-shore and walked along the continuation of the sea-wall towards the house-boat.

The dog was still there on the triangular piece of decking, looking as if it hadn't stirred since Rudd's previous visit. But the door in the super-structure was set open this time and, because the tide was full and the boat was riding high in the water, was almost level with the top of the dyke. Rudd had no difficulty in getting aboard and, stepping down inside the tiny cabin, found Thorpe sullen and unwelcoming, sitting on the bench, eating bread and jam, with a mug of tea on the floor between his feet. He had evidently not long got out of bed for he wore no shoes and his shirt was loose outside his trousers.

"You again?" he asked, as Rudd appeared.

"There's a few more questions I'd like to ask," Rudd replied cheerfully. He was feeling cheerful. Losing Stoll for a couple of days was like a weight being lifted off his back. He hadn't realised how much the man's continual presence had begun to haunt him. Besides, it was a fine day of young spring sunshine that, although it held no real warmth yet, was a promise of better things to come. Even the squalor of Thorpe's cabin seemed less oppressive on such a day and, with the door open, a lot of the stench had been dispersed. The Inspector felt he could breathe.

"You want a cup of tea?" Thorpe asked. He seemed to accept Rudd's arrival with a surly resignation.

"No thanks," Rudd replied promptly. Knowing something of Thorpe's habits, he guessed the mug in which it would be poured would be unwashed, or, at best, roughly swilled in river water.

"Suit yourself," Thorpe replied with a shrug. "You'll have to put up with me eating my own grub."

Rudd watched as the man ate and drank, wondering which would be the best way to approach him. A direct frontal attack? Or a subtle leading up to the crucial question? One thing was certain, he'd have to handle it carefully. Thorpe had only to deny that he'd been asleep that afternoon and the Inspector's carefully constructed set of suppositions would collapse like a house of cards. He guessed from the man's evasive answers to his questions on the previous visits that Thorpe was probably ashamed of what he had done. And he might very well go on lying and evading for the very powerful motive of protecting his own self-esteem.

When Thorpe had finished and wiped the back of his hand across his mouth, Rudd produced a packet of cigarettes, waiting until Thorpe had drawn deeply on his and seemed more relaxed. He had decided on the approach he would take.

"That last afternoon, when Melly visited you . . ." he began.

"Christ!" said Thorpe angrily. "Are you going over that bloody lot again! I told you . . ."

Rudd ignored him.

"She went for a walk," he continued, stating it as if it were an irrefutable fact.

Thorpe was silent. The statement had left him with nothing to say in denial. Rudd pressed home the advantage.

"She took the dog out after dinner," he went on.

"I wouldn't know," Thorpe mumbled. "Like I told you, she was out in the kitchen most of the time. I didn't see what she got up to."

"No, you didn't," said Rudd, "because, Mr. Thorpe, you were asleep, weren't you, in the living-room?"

Thorpe hesitated, avoiding the Inspector's eyes.

"I might a' been," he said at last. "I might a' dropped off for a while."

Rudd decided to leave it there. The admission that he had been asleep was enough. The fact that he had been drunk was not really relevant. Thorpe would have to come to terms with it in his own way and, if he chose to pass it off as a perfectly acceptable after-dinner nap, it was none of the Inspector's business.

"You have no idea where she went?" he asked.

"No," Thorpe replied. He was less on guard now that the question of his afternoon sleep seemed to have been accepted without too many awkward questions being asked. "She didn't say."

"Or if she met anyone on the walk?"

"No."

"Where might she have gone?"

Thorpe shrugged.

"I dunno. Through the village."

"No. She wasn't seen," Rudd replied. "Could she have gone down the lane?"

"She might."

It was like slowly squeezing an old, dry lemon, trying to get a few drops out of it.

"When she was a little girl," Rudd went on (not liking to say, "before your wife left you"), "did she ever take the dog for walks then?"

"Yes," Thorpe said reluctantly. He had averted his face and, from the expression of his profile, Rudd got the impression he was looking down a long, dark tunnel of memory at some small, bright image at the end of it. There was a desperate, peering intensity about the one eye in profile that Rudd could see.

"Where would she go?"

"I dunno. Anywhere. Across the fields."

"The fields at the end of the lane?"

"Yes."

There was a small silence and then he added, "She'd take a ball and let the dog run after it."

Rudd had a vivid mental picture himself of a little girl and a dog, joyously running across a meadow. Had Thorpe ever watched them? The girl was now dead and the dog was an old, sad mongrel whose only pleasure in life was to trail after Thorpe on his twice-daily visits to the local pub.

Rudd knew enough. There was no point in pursuing that line of inquiry any further. Besides, he had never enjoyed opening old wounds. He moved on to another subject.

"There's a creek that runs the other side of the sea-wall,

beyond the fields," he said in a matter-of-fact voice. "Is it navigable? Could you get a boat up it?"

"I dunno," Thorpe replied indifferently. "I live here"—and he jerked his thumb to indicate the house-boat—"but I don't know nothing about sailing."

"But boats do come past the village?"

"In summer, mostly. Week-enders. They keep their boats at Tolquay and places like that where there's boat-basins. But I've never seen them come close in-shore here-abouts. They keep to the channel further out."

"Because of the mud-banks?"

"I suppose so," Thorpe replied indifferently. It didn't seem a subject that interested him very much.

Rudd got up to go. Thorpe, still seated, watched as he buttoned up his overcoat.

"That man . . ." he began. There was no need for him to finish his sentence. The desperate eagerness in his face and voice, that Rudd had seen before, told the Inspector what the rest of the question would have been.

"Not yet," he replied gently.

As he stepped ashore, the dog roused itself and feebly wagged its tail, perhaps remembering Rudd from his previous visit and thinking of him as a friend. He took the trouble to bend down and stretch out a hand to pat its head. It seemed a small enough gesture to make but better than nothing. Then, turning away, he walked back to the village.

It was mid-morning and he had to decide what his next move would be. Although he was certain in his own mind that Melanie had left the cottage, where exactly she had gone and whom she had met, if anybody, remained unknown. Two words, however, kept running through his mind like recurring themes in a musical score: the word "transit" and the name "Eddy Lisle."

For the sake of nothing better to do, he drove back to Boxleigh, where he sat in the chintz and dark oak lounge of the White Hart, ostensibly drinking coffee and reading the *Daily Telegraph*, while he turned these words over in his mind, worrying away at them as a dog gnaws at a bone.

Eddy Lisle. There was still no positive connection between him and Melanie Thorpe, except what Bibby Tucker had heard the man shout out in his delirium and, since learning the details of the Lisle brothers' criminal career from Monk, there seemed to be no likelihood of a connection. An East End crook, serving a prison sentence for armed robbery and suspected of a string of similar offences, and a young, country-bred girl, a hairdresser's apprentice who was shy of boys; he couldn't imagine any tie-up between them. Melanie rarely left the village where she lived. The furthest she had gone was to Boxleigh, to work, or occasionally to the cinema. He had established this during the early inquiries, immediately after her death when he had been making up a list of her known friends and acquaintances. But it was just possible, he supposed, that they might have met.

The shop where she had worked was just down the road. He could easily call in and check again. She had been friendly with one of the other apprentices who might know if Melanie had ever gone up to London for the day. He hesitated calling on Melanie's mother, Mrs. Bridges, remembering her total collapse into grief when he had questioned her before. It was bad enough probing Thorpe's memory.

Monk's warning, too, remained in his mind: that Rudd's head would be for the chopping-block if he started inquiries into what was the Yard's special area of interest. Rudd realised he would have to tread very carefully when it came to asking questions directly connected with Eddy Lisle. Mere superiority of rank had never overawed him but he didn't want to run the risk of demotion or losing his job. Nor did he want to implicate Monk in any follow-up inquiries that might lead on from it. Monk had been, in some ways, talking out of turn. He had made it clear that what he had told Rudd had been unofficial "swap-shop" chat as he called it, exchanged on a friendly basis. Rudd couldn't, without risking Monk's career, use any of that information on Eddy Lisle without going officially through Scotland Yard channels, not that it seemed of much use anyway in his own inquiries into the murder of Melanie Thorpe.

There remained the other word, "transit," with its possible connection with navigation and boats. Merestead was near the sea. Dotted along the coast were yachting centres like Tolquay. It was possible that, if Melanie had taken a walk that Sunday afternoon along the sea-wall, she might have met someone who came by boat along the creek that, at high tide, seemed navigable.

On balance it seemed the best thread to follow, the one less likely to cause him to tread on any official toes.

Satisfied at having come to a decision, he lunched early at the White Hart and afterwards called briefly at Cheryl's, the hairdresser's shop where Melanie had worked, which was situated in the High Street, in order to check whether Melanie had ever been to London and might, therefore, have met Eddy Lisle there.

Melanie's friend, Denise, promoted now to qualified assistant and resplendent and almost unrecognisable in a complicated blond hair-do and iridescent eye-shadow, very different from the mousey, fifteen-year-old school-leaver who had scurried about cleaning wash-basins and fetching towels on his last visit, wasn't very helpful.

As far as she knew, Melanie had never been to London, not on her own, although she had spoken of occasional shopping trips with her mother.

"She didn't like London," Denise said. "She told me. I asked her several times to come with me for a trip up the West End on our half-day off but she wouldn't."

"Thank you," said Rudd, turning to go. That was one lead, at least, he had discovered wasn't worth following up. It would seem unlikely that Melanie had met Eddy Lisle on a visit to London.

Denise hesitated, the sophisticated veneer melting into an expression of genuine concern.

"Have you found him yet?" she asked. It was the same question that Thorpe had been so eagerly hoping for an answer to. "I still think of her, you know. I miss her."

Rudd shook his head, moved by her sincerity.

"Not yet," he told her. "But the case isn't closed."

He remembered her suddenly, standing by Melanie's grave, in a black coat obviously borrowed from an older woman, her mother perhaps, her face blanked out with tears.

Leaving the shop, he returned to the White Hart, where he put in a telephone call to the headquarters of the harbour police at Fairness. It seemed a more promising lead and the sergeant at the station was prepared to be helpful.

Yes, certainly, Detective Inspector Rudd was quite welcome to look at the charts of the area and to be taken on a launch along the coast.

"Any particular part you want to visit, sir?" he asked.

Rudd hesitated. He didn't want to give too much away at that state. It was like building up a construction brick by brick, and he wasn't certain himself what the final shape would be.

"Just south of Merestead?" he suggested. "And, by the way, do you keep tide-tables?"

"Yes, sir."

"Could you find out when it was high tide several years ago?"

There was a moment of surprised silence that the sergeant hastened to cover up.

"If you could give me the exact date, yes. I could look it up for you."

"April 3, four years ago," Rudd told him.

"Very good, sir. I'll have the information ready when you arrive."

"Thanks," said Rudd and rang off.

Fairness was a distance of some twenty miles away, an important town since it had become a tanker port. It was a sea-side resort as well, although Rudd had never seen its attractions as a pleasure centre. At this point along the coast, the marshes gave way to gravel beaches that, at high tide, presented the holiday-maker with a narrow and uncomfortable stony stretch on which to relax, packed in summer with recumbent bodies and deck chairs. At low tide, the water retreated, leaving behind a wasteland of odorous mud, littered with the trash left behind by the tourists, empty plastic bottles, beer cans and bits of rotting debris that even the sea rejected.

The splendid, deserted beauty of the salting at such places as Merestead no longer dominated the fore-shore. Instead a promenade ran the length of the sea-front, crowded with cheap cafes, bingo halls and amusement arcades, where the visitor could buy whelks and candy-floss, funny hats and picture post-cards, and cheap, plastic mementoes of a fortnight's happiness.

Beyond the beach, as a grim backcloth, reared the cranes and oil storage tanks of the port.

Rudd drove along the promenade to the harbour police headquarters, passing the shuttered shops and cafes. It was too early yet for the tourist season. The beach was empty, too, apart from a few local residents who were taking advantage of a walk on the beach before it became crowded with sun-bathers.

It was all sad and shabby. Even the sea seemed tamed, dawdling up to the shingle, as if bored by the whole business.

The harbour police headquarters lay at the far end of the promenade, towards the port, with its own little basin where launches were moored. Rudd entered the building, fairly new but already salt-scabbed, and was shown into Sergeant Duffy's office, where Duffy was waiting for him, a chart spread out in readiness on the table.

As they shook hands, Duffy said to him, "I've looked up the tide-tables for you, sir. It was high tide at 15:37 on the day you mentioned."

"Thank you," said Rudd, tucking that piece of information away in his mind for future consideration.

"And I've put out a chart that we can take with us if you want to," Duffy added.

"I'd like a look at it now," Rudd replied.

Walking over to the table, the two men bent down over it.

"I don't know if you know anything about charts," Duffy began in a diffident voice, torn between a desire to display superior knowledge and yet not appear too uppity in front of an officer of higher rank than himself.

"Not a lot," Rudd admitted cheerfully.

"These lines," Duffy said, pointing a finger, "indicate the high- and low-water points. The deep-water channels are shown as well."

"Yes, I see," Rudd said.

Although he listened with apparent interest, he was studying the chart from his own particular point of view. Unlike the Ordnance Survey map that he and Boyce had looked up, the chart showed the coast-line in much greater detail. He could follow it down from Fairness, past Tolquay and the other villages to Merestead. Some of the wider creeks were named. The one that lay just south of Merestead, and that poked into the countryside like a crooked finger, was called Mill House Creek, named, no doubt, from the farm that lay inland from it, just beyond the sea-wall, that was also marked in, called "Mill House Farm." Or perhaps the farm had been so named from its proximity to the creek. He had no doubt in his mind that it was the creek alongside which he had walked that morning from Thorpe's old cottage.

"I don't know quite what you're looking for," Duffy added. He was clearly longing to be taken into the Inspector's confidence and Rudd had no intention of doing anything of the sort.

"Just a few inquiries," he said vaguely. "They may lead nowhere."

To cover up the snub, he added quickly, "Tell me, do any private boats use Fairness as a centre?"

"Not now," Duffy replied. "Not since it's been turned into a tanker port. There's too many big boats around to make it safe. The local authorities have even stopped the pleasure boats from putting out too far into the shipping lanes. They can only operate inside the bay. If you're looking for a private basin, there's West Turnham or Tolquay further down the coast."

"Yes, of course," Rudd replied, as if it hadn't occurred to him. "And another small point," he added, making it sound of little consequence, "there's a word I've come across and I think it's got something to do with boats— 'transit.' "

"Oh, yes," said Duffy, eager to show he knew its meaning even if the Inspector didn't. "Transit points. They're a navigational aid, used by the owners of small craft, mostly. You pick out two points on the coast and when you've got a fix on them, when they're exactly in line, for example, you know you have to alter course, turn to port or starboard. Left or right," he added, in case this specialist jargon should be beyond the Inspector's obvious limited knowledge. He said it with the bright and helpful air of a patient schoolmaster explaining something abstruse to a small boy so that, despite his exasperation, Rudd couldn't help also feeling amused.

"Why?" he asked.

"Why?"

Duffy seemed surprised by the question.

"Why should anyone want to line up these transit points?"

"Oh, I see," said Duffy, getting the point. "Well, they could be used for several reasons, to avoid a mud-bank, for example, or some submerged hazard in the water, such as an old boat or even a plane. There's bits of several still lying out there from the second world war."

"Really?" said Rudd. "And what sort of things might be used as transit points?"

"Could be anything; a tree, say, or a church tower. Any object sticking up from the landscape that's always there, if you get my meaning."

"Yes," said Rudd. "I do. You've made it very clear. Thank you."

Duffy flushed with pleasure. Indicating the chart, he said in a self-conscious voice:

"Have you finished looking at it, sir?"

"Yes," said Rudd, "but I'd like to take it with me, if I may."

"Certainly, sir," Duffy replied, rolling it up with swift precision and snapping an elastic band round the resulting tube.

They made their way out of the building, collecting Bassett, a constable, on the way, who, Rudd gathered, was to be in charge of steering the launch, leaving Duffy free to answer the Inspector's questions.

At the edge of the basin, Duffy hesitated.

"You'll be all right getting aboard, sir?" he asked.

Rudd peered down the length of iron ladder, clamped to the side of the basin wall, to the launch that lay a perilous ten feet below him, bobbing about, moreover, with the movement of the water.

"Yes, of course," he said firmly.

All the same, they supervised his descent with the tender concern they might have shown an elderly lady.

I suppose, Rudd thought, as he thankfully felt the decking under his feet, that it wouldn't do for them to lose an inspector overboard. The question of protocol alone would present problems.

"Ready, sir?" Duffy was asking.

They were safely inside the wheelhouse.

"Yes," said Rudd.

Gazing through the glass at the gently heaving horizon, he added quickly and with no sense of shame:

"I'd rather you didn't go too fast."

He tried to ignore the amused glance that passed between the Sergeant and the Constable.

Very gently, the launch was eased out of the basin.

10

Once clear of the basin and out into open water, Rudd got used to the motion of the boat, although for the first quarter of an hour he was queasily aware of the lunch of lamb chops he had eaten at the White Hart too short a time before.

The shingle beach and port installations of Fairness slipped away behind them and then disappeared from sight as they followed the curve of the coast-line. The country-side reasserted itself, moving slowly past them to starboard; low fields and the occasional clump of trees, while, in the middle distance, along the shore-line, lay the green and brown flats of mud and marsh, glittering with water in the creeks and inlets. To port, the sea stretched out to the horizon but Rudd hardly looked at it. His eyes were turned towards the land.

There was little sensation of speed. Although the boat was moving fairly fast, it was keeping far enough out from the shore so that the view was distanced and seemed to pass slowly. He could see now, on an even larger scale, the inlets and creeks that cut inland, fretting the coast-line.

After half an hour of steady cruising, the marshes dropped back and a cluster of houses appeared on a wide opening of the sea, with boats, small white shapes at that distance, gathered like a handful of toys on the water.

"West Turnham," said Duffy, pointing to the chart that he had spread out for the Inspector to refer to.

Rudd put the binoculars that he had borrowed from the Sergeant to his eyes. The distant village leapt into closer focus. He could see the masts of the boats and the sheds that lined the fore-shore.

Then they were past the village and the marshes and fields took over once again.

It occurred to Rudd how small and isolated these coastal villages were; little islands of people and buildings in the open wastes of sea and marsh. In the rest of the country-side further inland there were more signs of occupation; an occasional farmhouse, a field of static black and white dots that he took to be cows; a distant line of telegraph posts that marked the presence of a road. But along the coast, the marshes were supreme, except for these tiny communities where people had come together perhaps thousands of years before, to huddle in protective clusters like people under siege.

"Tolquay coming up," the Sergeant announced.

Rudd again put the binoculars to his eyes, prepared, this time, for the startling change in distance.

"Take it slowly," he told the Constable at the wheel.

The launch idled past the village. The sea-wall here came close to shore, and the village, unlike West Turnham, was tucked away out of sight. He could, however, see some buildings along the shore that looked like boat-sheds, with craft moored near them. Behind them, more masts were poking up above the seawall, probably in some inner basin or small harbour. A pair of massive lock gates indicated this to be so.

"All right?" the Constable was asking.

"Yes," said Rudd, putting down the binoculars.

The village was passing out of sight behind them. He could always take a second look at it on the return journey. The launch had picked up speed again as they moved on down the coast.

Rudd glanced at his watch, noting the time. Twenty minutes later, the village of Merestead came into view.

"Slowly again!" ordered Rudd, the binoculars to his eyes.

It was strange seeing the village from this unfamiliar viewpoint. He caught a glimpse of Thorpe's house-boat, the black, shallow triangle of its roof, perched up above the marsh against the sea-wall. Then the houses began, running back from the foreshore, with the church tower poking up above the trees behind them. It suddenly occurred to him that it would make a good transit point. What had

Duffy said? "Any object sticking up from the landscape that's always there."

Well, the church was always there. But where was the second point?

"Can you get further in-shore?" he asked Bassett.

"I'll try, sir," the Constable replied. "But it's a bit tricky round here. There's a lot of mud-banks along this part of the coast."

Rudd remembered Thorpe saying that boats passing the village kept well out to sea and this was obviously the reason why Merestead had never developed as a yachting centre. Bringing a boat in-shore would be too hazardous.

He saw the second transit point at the same moment that he caught sight of the opening to Mill House Creek a little ahead. It was the end wall of a barn, painted white, but they were past it before he had time to line it up with the tower.

"Turn!" he ordered Bassett. "Go round and come back again."

The Constable obeyed and the launch turned out to sea, circled and came back again to the north of the village.

Rudd tried it this time without the binoculars. The view receded and widened, dropping back to its normal distance, but he could still pick out its main features, including the tower and the white wall of the barn. He watched them slowly shift position in relation to each other, moving into line, so it seemed.

"Slowly! Slowly!" he urged the Constable.

"Easy, lad."

The Sergeant added his own orders to Rudd's, sensing that whatever the Inspector had seen, it was something important.

The two points were almost lined up. A few more feet and they were.

Rudd looked quickly about him, as he faced in-shore. Slightly to his right lay the village. To his left were the marshes with the opening to Mill House Creek running inland, the sea-wall behind it and following its course. Beyond that, although he couldn't see it, was, he supposed, the field across which he had walked that morning, following the route that Melanie might have taken on the day she died.

The next second, when he glanced across, the tower and barn had shifted their positions and were no longer in line.

"Circle again," he told Bassett.

As they drifted past the village for the third time, he pointed to the creek.

"That opening . . ." he began.

"Ah, yes, sir. Mill House Creek," Duffy said with exasperatingly quick information.

"Could we get up it?"

The Sergeant hesitated.

"I wouldn't recommend it, sir. It's a question of finding our way into it across the mud-banks, especially now the tide's running out. We might finish up properly up the creek, if you see what I mean."

He laughed loudly at his own joke in which the Constable dutifully joined.

"But at high tide," Rudd persisted, "would it be possible to get a boat into it?"

Duffy looked doubtful.

"You might, sir. It depends. If there's a channel of deeper water running between the banks . . ."

"Is there one?" Rudd interrupted.

"Not that I know of," the Sergeant replied. "Of course, that's not to say there isn't. There's nothing on the chart, but not every channel's marked in, especially if it's a small one."

"So if there is a channel, someone could take a boat into that creek at high tide?" Rudd asked, trying to pin him down.

The Constable added his information to the Sergeant's.

"Someone must have done it at some time," he put in.

"Why?"

The question was asked by Rudd and the Sergeant almost at the same time.

"There's an old cement-bottomed lighter been dumped there," the Constable explained. "I've seen it myself at low tide. It's settled down in the mud, but a couple of inches of the top of it sticks up when the tide's out. God knows who put it there, but it must have been lying there for years."

"That's another reason why no-one would want to take a boat up there," the Sergeant said, a little snappishly. He seemed put out that the Constable should know something about the area that he didn't. "You could tear the bottom out of a boat if you went over that, not knowing it was there."

Perhaps it was the Sergeant's insistence that made Rudd pursue the point.

"But suppose someone did, would it be possible?"

The Sergeant drew in a deep breath before admitting reluctantly, "Well, yes, I suppose it could be, all supposing he didn't start off by getting himself stranded on the mudbanks."

"I don't know much about boats," Rudd admitted with assumed artlessness, as a sop to the Sergeant, "but what about getting out once he'd got in? The creek's not wide enough to turn a boat round in, is it?"

"No," agreed Duffy, somewhat mollified. "It can't be more than twelve feet across further in. It's wider at the mouth, of course."

He seemed suddenly to become interested in the hypothetical problem himself, for he said to the Constable:

"Turn back, Bassett, and let's have another look at her."

By "her," Rudd took him to mean the Mill House Creek. The launch circled again, approaching the village for the fourth time.

"If you could lend me the glasses, sir," Duffy asked Rudd.

With the binoculars to his eyes, he scanned the marshes as they drifted past the creek then, lowering them, said:

"Yes, I reckon you could get a boat in there. Not past that old lighter, though. It must take up quite a width of the channel. Getting out? Well, you could put the engine in reverse, I suppose. I take it you're thinking of a power boat of some kind, sir?"

"I'm not sure," said Rudd vaguely. "It's just an idea."

"It'd churn up a hell of a lot of mud," pointed out Bassett.

"That's true," agreed the Sergeant.

"You could pole the boat out, supposing you hadn't taken her in too far," the Constable added, with a bright, helpful air. He seemed to look on the problem under discussion as some sort of game, to be taken seriously on one level but treated, all the same, with a bit of tongue in cheek.

"Pole it out!" said the Sergeant disgustedly. "The mud's

feet deep in there, laddy, I wouldn't mind betting. You'd lose the pole before you struck bottom."

"I was thinking of poling it along by the sea-wall," the Constable explained in a subdued voice. "I've seen it done; one man on the stern, one aft."

"Pushing with a pole against the bank?" Rudd asked, interested.

"That's right, sir," Bassett said. He seemed unwilling to say more. Having been put in his place by the Sergeant, he was ready to retire from any further discussion.

"I see," said Rudd thoughtfully.

They had drifted past the opening of the creek while they talked.

"Do you want another look at her, sir?" Duffy was asking.

Rudd roused himself.

"No thanks," he replied. "I think I've seen all I want to see for the time being."

"We'll be pushing off, then, back to Fairness?"

"Yes," Rudd replied. "We can push off."

He was so silent on the way back that Duffy came to the conclusion that the Inspector was disappointed at the outcome of the trip. Whatever it was he had been looking for, he hadn't found it and Duffy felt obscurely guilty, as if he were in some way to blame.

In fact, Rudd was thinking deeply. A few more bricks had been added to his construction and, although he still had no idea what its final shape would be, he felt it was nearing completion. Exactly where Eddy Lisle fitted into it, he still had no idea, but he was beginning to realise that he would form a key-stone. If only he could slot him into place, the rest of it would follow.

At Fairness, having climbed gingerly out of the launch and thanked Duffy and Bassett, he drove out of the town, taking the road that led south to the coastal villages that he had already passed that afternoon by boat.

If a boat had played a part in the case, and he was beginning to think it had, because the word "transit" only made sense in that context, then it was possible it had come from either Tolquay or West Turnham.

From the police launch he had seen that both villages were popular yachting centres. The number of craft already moored there suggested this and the season had not

yet begun. But it had been April when Melanie Thorpe
was murdered and the yachting season then would not
have been properly under way. It followed, therefore, if a
boat had been used, it would more likely be one that had a
permanent winter mooring at one of the two basins.

He would have to make inquiries at both those places
but, meanwhile, there was something else he wanted to do
first: have another look at Mill House Creek, bearing in
mind what he had learned from Duffy and the Constable.

In Merestead he parked the car and walked once more
past Thorpe's cottage and across the field to the path that
ran along the top of the sea-wall. The tide was running out
and the water in the creek had fallen, revealing muddy
verges. One thing was certain, even to his inexperienced
eye, the creek would only be navigable at high tide.

He walked further on, passing the point where he had
halted and turned back on his last visit, supposing Melanie
had been gone from the cottage for an hour. It had been
only a rough estimate of the time, anyway.

The sea-wall curved to the right, following a bend in the
creek, and the marshes on the left widened out as they
neared the sea. The creek itself was broader, too, at this
point and, although the tide was ebbing, there was enough
mud left by the receding water to convince Rudd that a
smallish craft would have no difficulty in entering it at
high water.

After a further ten minutes' walk, he saw what he was
looking for: the rectangular iron rim of the abandoned
lighter just showing above the water on the landward side
of the creek. The bank of the sea-wall was steep and grass
that grew on it slippery, but he managed to slither down
the slope and, clinging to some of the longer tufts, felt
about a few inches above the water. He found, at last, what
he was looking for. Driven into the bank, a little distance
down-stream from the lighter, were two stakes, the first
quite close to it, the second about twenty feet away. They
were angled in such a manner that, from the top of the
sea-wall, they would be invisible among the long grass.

Mooring stakes. He remembered two similar posts
driven into the dyke on the far side of the village to which
Thorpe's house-boat had been tied by ropes fore and aft
and he had no doubt that these stakes had been put there
for the same purpose: to moor a boat in position near the

bank, just down-stream from the lighter, and prevent it from drifting over the lighter itself. He remembered Duffy's words, that it would tear the bottom out of a boat if it went over it.

He scrambled back up the bank and looked about him, familiarising himself with the area. Further down-stream still, the creek ran out towards the sea, surrounded now on both sides by marshes, for the dyke ran inland, curving like a protective arm round the pasture land that lay there.

At that distance, and without binoculars, it was difficult to pick out details, but he could make out the darker stretch of the creek as it opened out to meet the sea and the patches of shallow ripples that indicated the mud-banks that the water barely covered. There must be a deeper channel. There had to be. Someone had got a boat up there. The mooring stakes suggested this. And he thought he now knew why.

Mud. Several feet of it, according to the Sergeant. Soft and deep and yielding. You could lose a boat pole in it before you reached bottom. But a concrete-lined lighter, hidden at high tide and only just visible above the water-line at low tide, was a different proposition altogether. It must have settled down in the silt over the years and there was no risk of it sinking any further. It was there for good.

Should he call Monk? Rudd wondered. The trail seemed almost at an end. There were many loose ends still to be tied off, but he felt sure in his own mind that he knew the answer now to most of the questions. For instance, he knew the reason why she had been killed. The question of motive no longer puzzled him.

She had been out longer than he had at first imagined; an hour and a half, three quarters of an hour to reach the point at the sea-wall above where the lighter lay, the same amount of time to walk home, allowing time for the meeting to take place.

According to the Sergeant, high tide had been at 3:37 P.M. on the day she had been killed. Rudd did a few quick mental calculations as he walked back towards the village. She must have left the house at about a quarter to three, which allowed her time to wash up the dinner things and sweep the floor in the living-room, waking Thorpe up from his sleep as she did so. Supposing she had washed the kitchen floor immediately afterwards, taking the dog for a walk to get it out of the way while it was drying? She could have left the shirts soaking in the sink and been back in time to get them rubbed through and out on the washing-line for the neighbour to see them later in the afternoon, before Thorpe woke up.

These domestic details were not all that important, but it might prove vital later on in the case to prove that Melly had both the time and the opportunity to take that walk. Thorpe might have, in fact, been aware that she left the house and, although so far, he had only been prepared to admit that he had fallen asleep, Finch could probably force him into giving more detailed evidence, if he had to.

One thing seemed certain; she hadn't spoken to her father about the walk or who she had met or what she had seen. Possibly Thorpe was still surly after his boozy sleep or perhaps there was another reason why she had not mentioned it.

Other things, too, were becoming clearer but still lacked the certainty of proof.

Should he ring Monk? The question nagged away at the back of his mind as he walked back to the village. He knew he was reaching a crucial phase in the investigation and he'd have to watch every move he made. But this was his territory, after all. What did the men in London know of Essex or its people? Besides, wherever the Yard's interests lay, it was his case, too, and his concern was solving one small, local murder and not even the top brass in London were going to deprive him of the chance of doing it.

Start from the scene of the crime. It was an old police maxim. He had done it four years ago and gone back to it only the other day. But supposing, as he now believed, the trail started at Merestead and led, not inland, but along the coast? The lines of investigation now seemed to point to either Tolquay or West Turnham.

Rudd made up his mind. He'd continue working alone for a little while longer and, if he turned up something at either of those places, then he'd get in touch with Monk.

He rationalised the decision by convincing himself that, when it came down to brass tacks, he hadn't, in fact, a lot to tell him. There was the one word "transit" and its connection with Eddy Lisle. The rest of it was pure supposition. The fact that the church tower and the barn wall had lined up could be mere coincidence, while the mooring stakes might have some perfectly innocent explanation. It was all built on hunches, really, and he wasn't always right, as Boyce had pointed out to him. But, even as he thought it, he knew that, this time, he wasn't wrong.

As he walked past Thorpe's cottage, he paused at the gate for a few minutes. It was the place he most associated with Melly, more than the neat, red-roofed bungalow in Wiston. It was here that she returned, to the old life she had known for years, to her father and the old white mongrel dog that had been her pet. He had again the swift, vivid, mental picture of a little girl and a dog running across a meadow.

It would be an exaggeration to say he spoke to her. But, as he stood at the gate, gripping the top bar with both hands and looking down the length of the weed-grown garden to the derelict, clap-board cottage, he did seem to feel her very close, as a living presence; not as the huddled bundle of wet clothes and hair he had seen dumped in the edge of the field at Hadley Corner.

And he made her a promise, not in words but in a silent resolution, that he'd bloody well find the man who killed her and write "Case Closed" on the front of her file.

Turning away, his mind made up, he collected the car and drove away from the village along the Tolquay road.

11

Tolquay was a long, straggling village, hidden away behind the sea-wall, as Rudd had noticed from the police launch, and more self-consciously picturesque than Merestead. Some of the cottages that lined the road were clearly the week-end homes of the more affluent, prettied up with window-boxes and tubs of flowers, probably belonging to the people who used Tolquay as a yachting centre. There were other signs, too, of a more affluent community: an antique·shop and a ship's chandler's. Rudd stopped briefly to look in its window at the coils of nylon rope, the brass lamps, the baby anchors, the portable stoves and chemical lavatories; all the paraphernalia that went with owning a boat. Waterproof jackets and trousers, in bright orange and yellow, were hanging up at the back.

Turning away, he walked on. As he approached the far end of the village, the cottages gave way to boat-sheds and small wooden huts for the storing of gear. The dyke backed onto them, cutting off a view of the sea. Round the final bend, the road widened out into a large, hard-surfaced area, roughly circular in shape, fronted by more boat-houses and a public house, the Jolly Roger. Unlike the Anchor at Merestead, which was simply a village pub near the sea, the Jolly Roger had made the most of its sailing connections. A mast, looking out of place and land-locked, stuck out from the fore-court while ship's lanterns were fixed along the front of the building.

It was closed anyway, but Rudd doubted if, had it been open, he would have been tempted to go inside, knowing that the interior would contain the same type of sea-faring objects in the way of ships in bottles and paintings of the more attractive and romantic craft in full sail. He had an innate dislike for this kind of decoration. He preferred his beer in less elaborate surroundings.

The sea-wall continued round with a set of steps going up it, like those at Merestead, but better constructed, in concrete, with proper hand-rails. Masts were visible over the top of it on the sea side; craft, no doubt, moored along the fore-shore as he had noticed when he passed the village in the launch.

Mounting the steps, he stood on the top of the dyke, looking down on them. The tide had gone out even further, leaving them stranded on the mud, tilting at different angles. He looked them over, wondering what sort of craft he was looking for. It would be some sort of power-boat, he reckoned. A yacht would be too difficult to handle in a narrow channel, depending as it did on wind and sail.

There were about twenty boats moored there altogether and, as he looked down on them from the top of the sea-wall, he wished he knew more about sailing. Some were clearly out of the question, like the small dinghies and the yachts. Others were much too large to navigate the fairly narrow opening to Mill House Creek. There remained the boats, which he supposed were cabin cruisers and launches, and he realised he'd need to find out much more about them; for instance: What was the minimum amount of water they could safely operate in without getting grounded? Wasn't the proper word "draught"? He wasn't sure. One thing he was certain about, the boat wouldn't be much more than twenty feet in length. The distance between the mooring stakes in the bank at Mill House Creek suggested this.

To his right, the sea-wall ended at a pair of massive lock gates, behind which lay a basin in which more boats were moored. He remembered seeing through the binoculars on the launch masts sticking up behind those on the fore-shore and had guessed then that there must be some inland mooring.

The basin was large and contained more than forty boats, lined up three deep in places, waiting, no doubt, for the better weather and the sailing season to begin in earnest. Some were clearly wintering there, the curtains in the cabins closed, the open wells covered with tarpaulins.

Rudd sauntered past them, mentally dismissing, as he

had done on the fore-shore, those that seemed less likely. Even so, he was left with nearly thirty boats that might be the one he was looking for. There seemed to be no-one in charge of whom he could make any inquiries.

A long boat-house faced the basin, its doors open, so he knew somebody must be about. Walking across to it, he glanced inside. It was part work-shop, part show-room. At one end, a motor-boat was up on stands, a "For Sale" notice on its windscreen. At the other end, a smaller sailing boat was in the last stages of constuction. There was a pleasant, clean smell about the place of wood-shavings and varnish.

Opposite the open doorway in which he was standing, Rudd noticed another set of doors that seemed to lead out into some kind of private basin, perhaps the arm of a creek, for he could see a few boats tied up, a couple of masts sticking up and the super-structure of a cabin cruiser.

As he was looking, a young man in overalls came through the far doors and, seeing Rudd, walked over towards him.

"Can I help you?" he asked.

Rudd hesitated, wondering whether to walk away with some excuse. And then he decided to take the plunge. Why not? If he framed his questions carefully, he'd run little risk of rousing the man's suspicions.

"I was thinking of buying a boat," he said, deliberately assuming a diffident air. "And as I was in the district, I thought I'd call round and see if there was anything for sale."

"There's that," the man replied, indicating the motor-boat. "There's nothing else at the moment. It's a bit early yet in the season."

Rudd pursed his lips doubtfully.

"It's rather small," he said and laughed deprecatingly. "The wife had set her heart on something with a little cabin so that we could cook ourselves a meal on board."

The man looked him up and down.

"You don't know much about boats?" he suggested.

"No," agreed Rudd quickly. "But a friend's going to show me the ropes. It's his boat, really, that set my wife off wanting one. We thought of something in the cabin cruiser line."

As he was talking, he moved slowly towards the far set

of doors, looking about him as he walked, making it seem natural.

"The sailing round here's not for an amateur," the man was saying. "There's a lot of tricky shoals and currents offshore. You'd be better off keeping to the island water-ways or somewhere like the Broads."

"Oh, my friend would come with me the first few times out," Rudd replied.

He had reached the opening and was glancing out of it casually. He had been right in his assumption. The craft he had seen were moored in a small private basin, obviously belonging to the boat-builder's work-shop. He looked them over quickly as he spoke. Two were yachts and as such didn't interest him. The other was a cabin cruiser with the name *Mariette* painted in black letters on its white hull.

"I had in mind something more like that," he remarked, pointing to it.

As he did so, he noticed two things about it. One was the small winch that was bolted to the after-deck, close to the rails. The other was the long boat poles that were chained down along the length of the boat, two on each side of the cabin, in pairs, making four in all. Even though he knew little about sailing, it seemed to him that four poles were more than a boat usually carried.

"It's not for sale, is it?" he asked quickly, to cover up his obvious interest in it.

"Sorry, sir, no," the man replied.

"The owner wouldn't be open to offer?" Rudd persisted. "It's very much like the one my friend has that the wife fancied."

"I don't think so," the man replied. "The owner's never spoken about putting her up for sale."

"Pity," said Rudd. "It's just what I was looking for. Is the owner a local man? I might try getting in touch with him to ask if he'd be interested in selling."

"No, he's from London," the man replied. "I've got his phone number somewhere. I suppose it'd do no harm giving it to you. He might want to sell. He doesn't use her all that often. Hang on and I'll have a look."

Rudd followed him into the work-shop, where the man started looking through a pile of receipts and papers, fastened untidily together with a bull-dog clip.

"He gave me his phone number when the winch was

ordered. Asked me to take delivery of it and get it fitted on and let him know when the job was finished," the man was saying.

"Yes, I noticed the winch," Rudd replied with no more than a casual interest in his voice. "What's it for?"

The man shrugged.

"I dunno. He had some idea of trying to do a bit of salvaging from the wrecks off-shore. I don't think anything much came of it, as I could have told him, if he'd asked. There's not much money to be made out of salvaging unless you get a bigger vessel and the proper equipment. Ah, here it is."

He had unclipped from the bundle a small, grubby piece of paper with a telephone number on it.

"It's 01 407 5839."

"And the owner's name?" Rudd asked.

"Mr. Morrison."

Rudd kept his face blank as he jotted down the name and the telephone number in the back of his diary.

"Well, thanks," he said, putting it away. "It might be worthwhile giving him a ring sometime to see if he'll sell. If not, there's no special hurry."

"If you care to come back a bit later in the season," the man suggested, "I might have something myself for sale then."

"I'll do that," said Rudd and, nodding pleasantly, walked away, hiding his jubilation.

Morrison! It was the alias Frank Lisle had used, according to Monk, when he rented the warehouse in London.

On the drive back to the White Hart hotel at Boxleigh, he thought over the implications of what he had found out at Tolquay. If Morrison were indeed Frank Lisle, as Rudd had no doubt he was, a fact that could easily be verified by checking on the telephone number, then another link in the chain connecting the Lisle brothers with Melanie Thorpe had been established.

The significance of the four boat poles on board the boat puzzled him, however. Why four? Only two would be needed to pole the boat out of the creek, if that's what they'd done; two men pushing against the bank, one fore and one aft. So why the extra two? It was only a tiny detail, but it bothered him.

He waited until after dinner to ring Monk at home, preferring to make the contact with him a private and unofficial one at this stage, leaving it to Monk to put the information into official channels if he thought it worthwhile. Mrs. Monk answered the phone, saying she was sorry, her husband wasn't home yet.

"What time might he be back?" Rudd asked.

"I have no idea," Mrs. Monk replied, in the resigned tone of voice of a wife who has given up expecting to see her husband home at a reasonable hour.

"Could you get him to ring me at this number?" Rudd asked, giving her the number of the telephone in the hotel foyer. "Tell him it's important. I'll wait up for his call, however late. The name's Rudd, by the way."

He rang off and, going over to the reception desk, asked if he might borrow the L-R volume of the London telephone directory. As he had expected, a F.J. Lisle was listed as having the telephone number 01 407 5839.

He sat in the foyer, reading the newspapers and the copies of magazines that lay about on the low tables for the guests' use, listening for the telephone bell and watching the hands of the grandfather clock that stood in the corner and marked the passing of the hours with a slow, sonorous chime.

At ten o'clock, the other two guests had departed; a middle-aged man with a much younger girl, whom Rudd had already noticed in the dining-room. Illicit lovers, he guessed. But why choose Boxleigh as a rendezvous? Perhaps its very unlikeliness had been the reason. It was the last place a suspicious wife would come to look for an errant husband.

At eleven o'clock the managers began emptying the ashtrays and tidying up the cushions, a hint to Rudd that she considered it time he, too, retired.

"I'm waiting for a telephone call," Rudd explained. "It's rather urgent."

"What time are you expecting it?" she asked.

"I'm afraid I have no idea," Rudd replied, and added, embroidering quickly for her benefit, "It's a sick relative. Operation, you know. They could ring through any time."

"I see," she said doubtfully, only partly appeased, torn between sympathy and a desire to see the place properly locked up for the night before she went to bed.

"It's the lights," she explained. "I don't like leaving them on unless there's someone here to see they're properly switched off."

"Just the one reading lamp will do for me," Rudd replied. "I'll see it's turned off before I go to bed. And I won't pinch the spoons."

The last remark was a mistake, as he realised as soon as he said it. People waiting for urgent telephone calls about sick relatives weren't supposed to make jokes. She left but, from the doubtful look she gave him as she went up the stairs, he guesed she probably wouldn't sleep but would keep a watch on him from the landing upstairs.

It was a nuisance. The lounge and foyer, with the staircase leading up from it, were partitioned by beams only the plaster between having been removed to give a more spacious air. Anyone speaking on the telephone could easily be heard from above.

He read and smoked and waited, aware that every quarter of an hour a door was stealthily opened upstairs and a landing floor-board creaked. The manageress was on the prowl.

It was half-past twelve before the telephone finally rang. Rudd pounced on it before it had time to ring more than twice.

"Thank God you called," he said. "I've been so worried about Edna."

"Edna?" said Monk's voice. "Is that you, Rudd? What the hell are you on about?"

"Yes, it's ine."

"Oh, I get it. You're somewhere where you can be overheard."

"Yes. I'm so glad she's all right," Rudd replied.

"Okay. I get the idea. I'll read between the lines," Monk told him.

"I'll be coming up to see you first thing tomorrow," Rudd went on.

"Officially this time?"

"If you think it necessary."

"The Lisle brothers again?"

"Yes, and could you arrange it so that we talk alone. There's a lot to discuss about Edna and you know how uncle likes to interfere."

"I take it by 'uncle' you mean the top brass?"

"Exactly," said Rudd. "If we could chat about Edna

first, before consulting uncle, then we could get things sorted out between ourselves. You know, about her investments and things like that. Now she's in hospital, someone will have to handle them."

"Hang about!" said Monk excitedly. "If I read you right, Edna's Eddy Lisle, the hospital's Parkgate prison and the investments are . . ."

"All that money she so carefully put away for her retirement," Rudd said mournfully.

"Christ!" said Monk. "You can't mean it?"

"I think so," replied Rudd. "That's why we must talk first. We don't want uncle realising we've gone behind his back on certain matters. And then there's Mr. Morrison to take into consideration."

"Morrison? Frank Lisle?"

"Exactly," said Rudd.

He heard a board creak on the landing near the head of the stairs and added quickly, "I'll see you first thing tomorrow. And I'm so relieved that Edna's going to be all right."

He rang off smiling and, switching off the light, mounted the stairs, carefully rearranging his features in case he should meet the manageress. But she had heard him coming and had already whisked out of sight.

Sitting up in bed, he remained awake thinking. The central arch of his construction had almost come together. Only one more piece was needed, the key-stone to the arch: the identity of the man who had killed Melanie Thorpe.

It was one of the Lisle brothers, of this he was now certain, for he thought he knew what had happened on that last afternoon spent at Merestead. She had walked across the field with the dog, climbed the sea-wall that ran alongside Mill House Creek. She had seen the boat moored below. The tide was high. The lighter would not have been visible above the water. She had seen, though, what the men on board were doing although she probably hadn't realised its significance. But, as far as they were concerned, she was a dangerous witness who had to be got rid of.

Eddy Lisle was almost certainly one of those men. The other could have been his brother Vic. As Monk had said, they were close, they made a pair.

What happened then, he wasn't certain. Somehow they must have found out where she lived and her movements later in the day. Had one of them followed her home? It

seemed unlikely. The village was small. The presence of a
stranger would almost certainly be noticed and no-one had
seen anyone out of the ordinary on that Sunday afternoon.
The initial inquiries had proved this. Nor had she been
accompanied on the homeward journey on the bus. The
conductor had been certain about this. She had travelled
alone, as she had done on the way to Merestead in the
morning.

Nor was it likely, from the questions he had asked of
Denise, her friend at the hairdresser's, that the meeting was
prearranged. Melanie had not met the Lisle brothers on
any trip to London. If she saw them that afternoon, it must
have been for the first time.

What then had ahppened? She was a shy girl. It seemed
unlikely that she would stop to talk to two unknown men
unless there was something in their personalities that had
disarmed her. He wished he knew more about them. Monk
had told him so little that he had no picture of them in
mind to help him.

Had they chatted her up? Had they arranged later to
give her a lift part of the way home?

It seemed a possibility. Eddy Lisle had called out the
name "Melly" in his delirium. It was the pet name by
which she had been known among the family. She could
only have given it to him herself.

The words "Rudd" and "Essex" he could have heard
from another source. Assuming the Lisle brothers were
concerned in her murder, they must have kept an anxious
watch on the local newspapers, following the course of the
investigation from their reports. It must have come as a
great relief to them when the paper no longer carried any
accounts and the case seemed to be abandoned.

The word "transit" must have been on Eddy's mind for
another reason. If Rudd's theory was correct, he would be
keyed up, watching for the tower and the barn wall to
come into line, before manoeuvring the boat through the
channel. With the cargo they were carrying, they didn't
dare risk grounding it on the mud-banks. Eddy must have
found that the most nerve-racking part of the journey.

There were more details to be sorted out; the reason
why the girl's hand-bag had been rifled, for example, or
why they needed four poles on board the *Mariette*, but

now he had the broad pattern in his mind, these were details that would fall into place later.

His main concern was getting evidence. The Yard would be largely concerned with closing their own files on the Lisle brothers, although if he played his cards right, he could probably count on their co-operation. But his would be the main responsibility of seeing that the charge of murder was brought against the right man.

What had he got so far? Very little, he decided, and most of what he had was circumstantial, if not mere supposition. There were no finger-prints, no witnesses, at least none he had found so far; nothing that he could take into court. No jury would convict any of them on the little he had to offer.

It was, as Boyce kept pointing out, a question of facts. The trouble was, after four years, the facts tended to be forgotten or covered over.

Rudd punched up his pillows and tried to sleep. He was going up to London the following day to meet Monk and, no doubt, some of the top brass, officially for the first time. And he'd probably need all his wits about him for that.

12

The next morning, Rudd met Monk at the Yard in a little, cramped office where they were unlikely to be interrupted and the Inspector recounted the events that had happened so far, starting with the murder of Melanie Thorpe, the tailing of himself by Stoll, the interview with Bibby Tucker and his own inquiries at Parkgate prison that had convinced him that Eddy Lisle was in some way involved.

Monk, who had been listening with his small, brown eyes alive with interest, interrupted him at this point to ask, "And that's when you first arranged to see me, to ask about the Lisle brothers?"

Rudd nodded.

"At that stage I had no idea there were four of them, although the name Eddy Lisle seemed familiar and, of course, I learned at Parkgate he was in for armed robbery. It seemed an unlikely lead at the time and, since you'd warned me I'd be messing about with something big, I tried another line of inquiry, following up the word 'transit' and its possible connection with boats and navigation."

He went on to explain the theory as to how a boat could have been taken up Mill House Creek and how Melanie Thorpe might have seen it and been murdered because of it.

"And then, yesterday," he continued, "I poked about at Tolquay and saw a boat, complete with winch and boat poles, and was told it belonged to a Mr. Morrison, with this phone number."

He passed his diary to Monk, who immediately reached for the directory on his desk.

"Don't bother," Rudd told him, "I've already checked. It

belongs to an F. J. Lisle of Queenswood Road, Southwark."

"Frank Lisle," said Monk softly.

"That's what I thought," said Rudd. "But let me get back to my theory, and it is only a theory. I think Eddy and possibly Vic took that boat into Mill House Creek the day Melanie Thorpe was murdered. They were using the winch to lower something heavy off the boat into the lighter. I didn't have time to get a good look at it when I called at Tolquay yesterday. I was passing myself off as a prospective buyer, a bit green, which I am anyway, and I didn't want to rouse the suspicions of the man at the boat-builder's by showing too much interest in that one particular cabin cruiser. But I think, from the quick look I did get, that it's a power winch that probably runs off the engine. They'd need it, wouldn't they, if my guess is right? Because what they'd be lowering into that lighter would be fairly heavy; strongly built, waterproof steel boxes to withstand the corrosion of seawater over several years. And the lighter, of course, would be the ideal place to put them. Those creeks are feet deep in mud but the lighter has a concrete bottom. The boxes would sink only as far as its depth. They'd be sure of retrieving them sometime in the future."

"Three quarters of a million pounds' worth of loot," said Monk softly. His eyes sparkled at the thought of it.

"It's a good place to stash it," admitted Rudd. "No other boat would be likely to use the creek because of the mud-banks. The place is quiet; the village some distance away. They were unlikely to be seen. If Thorpe hadn't drunk himself asleep that afternoon and Melly hadn't taken the dog for a walk across that field, we still wouldn't know where they'd hidden it."

And she'd still be alive, he added silently to himself.

"Dates!" said Monk. "We'll need to fit this in with what we know of the Lisle brothers' activities. What day was it this girl died?"

Rudd told him and Monk made a few rapid calculations on a piece of paper.

"I'll need to check the exact dates from the file," he said, "but, working on a rough estimation, that was shortly after the series of bank-raids."

"So they must have been back since," Rudd pointed out, "with the stuff they got from the other hold-ups, the dia-

mond merchant's and the bullion dealer's." He paused and
then added, "Look, Reg, I'm going to leave it to you to
decide what you do with this theory. Talking to you that
day in the Rose Tavern puts us both on the spot, but you
more than me. Officially, I'm not supposed to know anything about the Lisle brothers, except for the one bit I
turned up myself in Parkgate prison. Obviously, the top
brass will have to be brought in on this but I don't want to
risk your career for passing on information, especially if
they take the line, as they may do, that you should have
insisted I come to them with what I knew at that early
stage. The point is, I've got my own case to solve: that
girl's murder and, as far as I'm concerned the Yard's inquiries are none of my business, except where they cross
mine. What do you think, Reg? Make a clean breast of it?
Or blur over the edges a bit and make it look as if this
meeting we're having now is the first time I found out
about the Lisle brothers' activities?"

Monk looked at him and grinned.

"What do you think?"

"I'd say, blur it over. It's simpler that way. The story
gets told as a straightforward account in the same way as
I've told you today. It's only confusing the issue to muddle
it up with questions of procedure and protocol, especially if
it puts you, and to a certain extent me as well, on the hot
seat."

"I agree," Monk said, and added with a laugh, "but only
because you've got the face for it. Nobody would dream of
doubting that frank, open look of yours. Anyway, I can't
see myself that it's worth it. You've proceeded quite legiti-
mately. I've only chatted. As long as they get the Lisle
brothers and recover the loot, I don't see they have anything to grumble about."

"It's only a theory," Rudd pointed out. "The evidence,
apart from what you may find at the bottom of that lighter,
is nil. We know Frank Lisle owns a boat, but so what? So
do hundreds of other people. The existence of some deep-
water channel between the mud-banks into Mill House
Creek is only supposition so far. So is my idea that Bibby
Tucker overheard that conversation in Parkgate prison
hospital. I haven't proved it."

"We could pull him in for questioning," Monk pointed
out.

"When you do, I want to be there," Rudd said quickly. "And there's one other point that I'll make now and I'll make again to anybody else, however high up the ladder they may be; my main concern is finding Melanie's killer and bringing him to trial. I'm quite certain in my own mind it was one of the Lisle brothers. Which one has yet to be proved."

"Could be any of them," Monk said. "They're all ruthless enough to have done it."

Catching sight of the expression on Rudd's face, he added quietly, "You really mean it, don't you? Nailing her killer is important to you?"

Rudd made a small gesture with one hand.

"I get involved in some cases. Personally, I mean. I know I shouldn't but I saw her lying in those nettles . . ."

"I know," said Monk with quick understanding, "and I'll back you on this one to the top."

Glancing at his watch, he added briskly, "Look, I'd better get the brass in on it. It'll take time but they're certain to want to see you. Do you mind hanging about in here until they get themselves sorted out?"

"All right," said Rudd. "I'll wait."

He waited for over an hour before Monk came back.

"They're ready for you," he announced. "I've filled them in with a brief account but they want to hear the details from you. There's a couple of Detective Chief Inspectors, Mace and Wylie; Detective Superintendent Ross and Detective Superintendent Harvey, who'll be in charge of the meeting. Watch out for Ross. He's the one with the iron-grey hair and the granite profile. He's what he looks, a hard, mean man. If anyone asks awkward questions, it'll be him."

He added as they walked down the corridors, "They're excited. I can tell. Even Ross raised his eyebrows, which in anybody else'd be a full attack of hysterics."

The office where the conference was held was large and comfortable, with a gleaming desk behind which Harvey was sitting. A semi-circle of chairs was arranged in front of it.

Harvey shook hands with him and introduced him to the other police officers already present. Rudd glanced quickly into their faces, picking out the ones who might be sympathetic. Only Ross returned his glance with a quick, hard stare that Rudd didn't much care for.

"If you'd like to be seated, gentlemen," Harvey was saying, and the group settled itself on the chairs, Monk among them. Rudd was glad he was to remain. He might need his help if the conference turned awkward.

As they sat down, Rudd noticed a police stenographer slip quietly into the room and place himself at the back. So it was all going to be officially recorded.

"Detective Chief Inspector Monk has already given us a brief account," Harvey said, addressing Rudd, "but we'd like to hear it again from you."

"Certainly, sir," said Rudd promptly and retold what he had already said to Monk but in more formal language.

It was when he reached the stage of his visit to Parkgate prison that the first interruption came from Ross.

"When was this, Inspector Rudd?" he asked sharply.

"I'm afraid I can't remember the exact date," Rudd replied. "As I've explained, I haven't been using my office recently as Stoll has been tailing me and I wasn't able to look up my notes."

"But that was the first time you heard the name Eddy Lisle mentioned?" Ross persisted.

"Yes," said Rudd brightly, "although at the time it didn't mean a lot to me. Inspector Monk has since told me this morning something of the Lisle brothers. Of course, as I explained to him, I haven't yet got any definite proof that it was Eddy Lisle that Tucker overheard."

"I've suggested that we pull Tucker in for questioning," Monk put in. "Detective Inspector Rudd has some idea where he might be found."

"I think that can be decided later, when we've worked out a more general strategy," Mace said.

"I agree," Harvey added.

The awkward moment seemed to have passed. Across the semi-circle Monk made a tiny, conforting signal by flickering his eyes and Rudd relaxed.

"If you'd like to resume," Harvey was suggesting to him.

Rudd took up the account again. He was on easier ground now, his own territory. He explained how he had followed up the line of investigation suggested by the word "transit" and how it had led him to Tolquay and to the discovery of the cabin cruiser *Mariette* owned by Mr. Morrison.

"Which I gather this morning," said Rudd blandly, "is an alias used by Frank Lisle."

"It fits," Monk put in quickly. "It checks with the telephone number that Inspector Rudd was given at the boatbuilder's yard."

Even Ross didn't take that up. It was Wylie who asked: "Any risk the man at the boat-builder's might warn Frank Lisle?"

"No," said Rudd firmly. "As far as I could see, he took me simply as someone interested in buying a boat. I said I'd get in touch with Mr. Morrison myself. It was the winch that attracted my attention in the first place. It seemed an odd thing to have on a small cabin cruiser. The man said Morrison was interested in salvaging but it didn't seem a very likely explanation. I've realised since, of course, what it could have been used for."

He glanced across at Monk, inviting him to take up the account, which he promptly did.

"It's only a theory, but we think it may have been used to lower water-tight boxes into the lighter. I've checked the dates. Inspector Rudd's inquiries into the death of this girl, Melanie Thorpe, pinpoint April 3, four years ago, the day she died. This would be only a few days after the raid on the bank in Luton."

"So it's likely they've been back since, after the other holdups?" Mace suggested.

"I don't know," said Rudd. "I have no evidence on that. I've been following my own inquiries into the girl's murder. It seemed likely that she'd met somebody on that walk, someone who came by boat, as the mooring stakes suggested, but I've got no proof."

He paused and, taking a breath, added, "I'd like to get that proof, if I can."

A slight rustle spread through the group, the police officers rearranging their legs and glancing at each other. Behind the desk, Havey said blandly:

"We'll do our best to help, Inspector Rudd, but I feel it's something we can discuss at a later stage."

"Very good, sir," Rudd replied, without letting his face betray his thoughts.

"We've got to decide what move we're to take first," Harvey went on, addressing the group in general. "I suggest that, for a start, Inspector Rudd take a few of you over the territory, to familiarise you with the places he's mentioned." He glanced down at his notes and added, "Merestead and Tolquay."

"I would suggest you restrict your inquiries in Tolquay," Rudd put in. "If several of you turn up, inquiring about the *Mariette*, the boat-builder may get suspicious and ring up Morrison—Frank Lisle, that is. The boat's kept in his private basin. I got the impression he was looking after it for Lisle when it wasn't being used."

"A good point," said Harvey approvingly. "We'll keep a low profile there."

"But there'd be no harm in looking round Merestead," Rudd went on. "As I told Chief Inspector Monk, my whole theory depends on the existence of some deep-water channel between the mud-banks. That'll have to be checked on."

Harvey looked at Mace.

"See that the river police get on to that," he told him. Mace nodded and made a note on the pad he was holding on his knee.

Harvey turned to Rudd.

"You say this creek is only navigable at high tide?"

"Yes, as far as I know," said "Certainly, it would be easier to get a boat in there when the creek's full. The winch is on the after-deck so they'd need to approach the lighter stern first. If Bassett, the Constable at Fairness, is correct, and he seemed to know a fair amount about boats, they'd pole the boat along the bank, one man on the stern, one man in the prow."

"Two of them!" said Harvey, almost to himself. He was silent for a moment and then went on, addressing the group as a whole, "I don't know what you think, gentlemen, but it seems we have here an opportunity for getting both Frank and Bunny in the bag. Supposing we leak some information to Frank Lisle that would panic him into trying to recover the stolen property from this lighter? It would have to be carefully timed so that we were ready to go into action the moment he made a move. If what Inspector Rudd has now told us, that there'd have to be two of them to handle the boat, the chances are he'd send for

Bunny Lisle, who, as far as we know, is somewhere abroad. I don't think he'd risk bringing in an outsider."

There was a suppressed buzz of excitement among the group, individuals turning to each other with whispered comments.

Harvey tapped on the table.

"Do I take it that we are in general agreement?" he asked.

There were nods of approval.

"Very well." He turned to Rudd. "We'll keep in touch with you as our plans are developed," he said, "and, of course, you won't need telling that anything you have heard here this afternoon is in the strictest confidence."

"Of course, sir," said Rudd primly.

"Are there any further questions you'd like to ask Inspector Rudd before the conference is over?" Harvey asked.

Wylie leaned forward.

"I'd like Inspector Rudd to go over once again the significance of the transit points," he said.

Rudd explained again, adding, "If my theory is correct, they'd use them to find their way through the deep-water channel."

"But with the winch in the stern, they'd need to come in stern first. Wouldn't that be difficult if they had to keep these transit points directly in line?"

"They could turn the boat in the mouth of the creek, I suppose," replied Rudd. "From what I can remember, the water looked deep and fairly wide there."

"So when they're ready to leave, they'd have the prow of the boat pointing out to sea," said Wylie with the air of a man who has satisfactorily dealt with a problem.

"Yes," said Rudd.

He imagined the scene. The creek, as he had seen it; a boat, the *Mariette*, tied fore and aft to the steep bank of the dyke, its white prow pointing towards the wide stretch of darker water where the creek ran out to join the sea between the grey and brown marshes. And somewhere inland, out of sight now behind the dyke, the tower of the church and the white wall of the barn, diminished by distance and almost lost among the surrounding trees.

It was, then, that he saw the significance of the second pair of boat poles. Of course! With the transit points behind them, they'd need some sort or marker to indicate the channel for the return journey. Two poles, driven into the deep mud, would serve as guides on their way out. They would steer the boat between them, retrieving them as they passed safely through them.

Harvey was looking at him.

"You seem about to say something, Inspector Rudd," he remarked.

Rudd explained quickly, adding, "I noticed them at the time and thought it strange the boat carried two sets of poles. If I'm correct, that's what they were used for."

"And another piece of evidence supporting your theory," Harvey replied. He looked round the group. "Are there any more questions or points that you wish to raise?"

Monk indicated he would like to speak.

"It occurred to me that if we do pull Tucker in for questioning, we could use him as the tip-off for Frank Lisle."

"It's an idea," agreed Harvey. "But I don't want Tucker touched until we're good and ready. There's a lot of preliminary work to be done first. We've got to check on that deep-water channel. We'll need to find out when it's high tide along that coast at the best time to suit us. I shall want detailed maps and charts of the whole area. And meanwhile, I want a twenty-four-hour surveillance kept on Frank Lisle until we're ready to move."

"There's Stoll, too," Rudd pointed out. "I don't think he knows much and he's not likely to tip off Frank Lisle. If I read his mind right, he was hoping I'd lead him to the proceeds of the Lisle robberies. But he knows enough to make him a potential danger."

"Where is he now?" Harvey asked.

"Probably still following Miller around," Rudd said with a smile. He had already explained Stoll's part in the case and how, using Miller, he had been able to give him the slip. "If I go on using the White Hart at Boxleigh, he's not likely to pick up my trail but he may spot Miller and get suspicious."

"I don't want him picked up yet, either," Harvey said. "It's up to Miller to see he doesn't get suspicious. See that that's made clear to him, Inspector Rudd."

"Very good, sir," Rudd replied.

It looked as if Miller would have to go on sleeping at his

house and he wondered if Dorothy really minded. But it was a small price to pay when the stakes were so high.

"Well, gentlemen," Harvey was saying, clearly ready to conclude the conference, "if there're no other questions, we'll leave it there for the time being. I suggest Monk and Wylie accompany Detective Inspector Rudd on a preliminary inspection of the area. You'd better put up at the same hotel he's using. And meanwhile the rest of us can start working out some plan of action. I'll call a further conference later."

He began rising from his chair as Rudd spoke.

"There's one point, sir, that I'd like to raise," he said firmly. "It's about my own case, the murder of Melanie Thorpe. I'd like to have any information on the Lisle brothers that might lead to the conviction of one of them."

There was a small silence and then Harvey said, "Of course. It's in our interest, too, if one of them could be charged with murder. I'll see to it that any information is available to you."

"Thank you," said Rudd, and he meant it.

The meeting broke up, Monk and Rudd accompanying Wylie to his office, where they discussed their own parts in the coming official inquiries. It was decided that Rudd would return to the White Hart hotel and book rooms for the other two men, who would join him later. Rudd then rang Boyce to tell him Miller was to resume his impersonation of himself.

"And tell him he's not to let Stoll rumble him," he warned.

"I'll pass the message on," said Boyce. "How's it going?"

"All right," said Rudd cautiously.

"Where are you?"

"In London," Rudd told him and left it there.

He knew he ought to telephone Dorothy as well, to let her know Miller would be returning but decided to leave it until he got back to the White Hart.

"I think the conference went well," Monk remarked as they left Wylie's office, "although, for a moment, I thought we were going to have a sticky time with Ross asking too closely about the exact dates you'd found out certain information."

"So did I," Rudd admitted. "What time do you and Wylie expect to arrive in Boxleigh?"

"Early evening?" Monk suggested. "I've got some stuff on my desk I must clear up first."

"I'll push off now," Rudd said. The conference had left him tired and he was hoping for an hour or two's rest before he had to begin again.

He drove back to the hotel, rang his sister and then booked rooms for Monk and Wylie. Then, after a few seconds' thought, he left the hotel and went to a public telephone where he put through a call to Superintendent Davies at headquarters with a request for a certain line of inquiry to be followed through. In the foyer on the way back he was met by the manageress, who asked:

"How is your relative?"

"Relative?" asked Rudd, for a moment at a loss as to what she meant.

"The one who was ill and you waited up for the telephone call about."

"Oh, she's much better, thank you," Rudd assured her and, stepping past her, went upstairs before she could ask him any more questions. In his bedroom, he stretched himself out on the bed and slept heavily for a couple of hours.

Monk and Wylie arrived later in the evening, in time for drinks in the bar before dinner but too late to look round the area.

"We'll make an early start tomorrow," Rudd told them. "It's too dark now to see anything, but I've bought some large-scale maps and charts and we can look those over this evening. They'll give you some idea of the lay-out of the places."

The following morning they set off by car, Rudd having traced for them the evening before the route they would follow.

It was a strange experience taking them over the same ground that he had already covered so many times, seeing the same places through their unfamiliar eyes. They stopped briefly at the gate opening at Hadley Corner, where Rudd pointed out the place where Melanie's body had been found, but he could tell by the cursory glance they gave it, that they were not involved in the case in the same way he was.

At Merestead, he parked the car and led the way past

Thorpe's cottage and across the field to the sea-wall, where they walked in Indian file along the path. There was no-one to see them, only some cows in the pasture that stared at them for a short while and then went on placidly feeding.

"Bleak place," commented Wylie, looking about him with a Londoner's eye. Rudd felt obscurely angry that he couldn't see the desolate beauty of the place; the vast expanses of sea and sky, the subdued and subtle colouring of marsh and water.

The tide was running in but the outline of the lighter was just visible below the surface, a dark oblong about eighty feet long and twenty feet wide. Rudd pointed it out to them and the position of the mooring stakes in the bank.

Wylie grunted and, lifting the binoculars he had brought with him to his eyes, studied the marshes and the far water where the creek opened out into the sea.

"Yes, you're right," he said after a few minutes' silence "there's enough room there to get a boat in and turn it. And I can see what you mean about the mud-banks. There's no sign of a channel but I suppose there must be one."

He turned to Monk.

"What do you think about placing men here?" he asked. "There's no cover worth speaking of but I suppose if we positioned them below the sea-wall, they wouldn't be visible to a boat approaching along the coast."

Monk agreed.

"And we could have a couple of launches standing by out to sea."

"They'd be spotted," Rudd pointed out. "It's too early in the season for many boats to be about. If Frank Lisle sets off from Tolquay in the *Mariette*, which I suppose you're counting on him doing, he's certain to notice them and get suspicious."

Wylie smiled.

"Leave us to worry about that," he told Rudd. "We'll see it's handled properly."

As a detective chief inspector he seemed to have assumed charge of the inquiry and to treat Rudd as a local man whose territory hadn't got a lot to offer, anyway. Behind his back, Monk dropped one eyelid at Rudd in an amused wink.

"Well," said Wylie, a little huffily, as if he'd been brought there under false pretences, "there doesn't seem much else worth looking at. Shall we move on?"

They drove on to Tolquay, Rudd remaining in the car while the other two men had a look round the village. The man at the boat-builder's had already seen him and he didn't want to run the risk of being recognised.

Wylie and Monk were gone for half an hour. They came back looking nipped by the wind and Wylie got thankfully back into the car, slamming the door shut after him.

"We've had a look at the main basin," Monk told Rudd, "and we've seen where the creek runs into it through a small lock behind the boat-builder's place. Unfortunately, it was locked up so we weren't able to get a look at the cabin cruiser. I suppose, if Frank Lisle wanted to shift it, he'd have to bring it down through the small lock into the basin and then through the main lock to put it out to sea?"

"Or the man at the boat-yard may do it for him," Rudd pointed out. "It's something you can check on later. As I said, I got the impression when I called there myself that the man at the yard probably looks after the boat for Lisle. He certainly fitted the winch on for him, and he may maintain it as well; see it's filled up with fuel for a trip, for example."

"In that case," Wylie remarked, "if we think he's willing to be co-operative, he could tip us off when Lisle's ready to move. That way, we'd be sure of having at least a few hours' warning to get ourselves into position."

He spread out the map over his knees.

"What do you think, Monk? One mobile headquarters in Tolquay, another at Merestead? A couple of launches positioned somewhere along the coast. Men stationed at the sea-wall. The coast road's closed, just in case they try to make a break for it. It's going to be quite an operation. God knows how many men we'll need."

"Let Harvey worry about that one," Monk replied.

"We'll get the river police set up, too," Wylie went on. "I'd like a look at it myself from sea. And another thing . . ."

Rudd remained silent on the drive back to Boxleigh, letting Wylie and Monk do all the talking. He felt this part of the case had already been taken out of his hands. Not that he minded. It wasn't his responsibility and he was glad to be out of it. But he did, however, feel Wylie was deliberately excluding him and he was human enough to feel resentful of his attitude.

Before the two men left to return to London, Monk managed to get Rudd on his own.

"I'll keep you in the picture," he told him and added, after a moment's hesitation, "I hope Wylie didn't put you out. He's an efficient devil but a bit short on tact sometimes."

Rudd smiled, acknowledging the apology offered by Monk on Wylie's behalf, but feeling less warm towards the man himself and even less so when he discovered he had departed with the Ordnance Survey maps and charts that Rudd had the day before bought out of his own pocket.

He hung about the hotel for several days, unable to go far in case Monk should ring him. He looked at magazines and drank coffee and thought about the Thorpe case, without coming up with any new ideas, and he telephoned Boyce one morning, in order to find out what was happening with regard to Stoll.

"He's still following Miller about," Boyce told him. "It's even beginning to get Miller down. He says he's been tempted more than once to give him the slip."

"Tell him he's not to lose him under any circumstances," Rudd said firmly. "Things could be warming up here any time and I want to know where Stoll is—that is, on Miller's tail."

"About that other inquiry," Boyce went on. "The Super's passed it on to me, and I'm following it up. No joy yet but I'm living in hopes."

"Good," said Rudd.

The manageress appeared at the desk and he rang off at this point, anxious that she shouldn't overhear too much of his official calls.

He rang Dorothy next, more for the sake of something to do but partly, as he had to admit to himself, out of guilt that he was making use of her. But she sounded perfectly happy with the situation. Mr. Miller was a very pleasant man, she told him, and he'd mended the electric kettle for her. Which was more than I've done, Rudd thought as he rang off.

Three days later, Monk rang him, sounding jubilant.

"We're moving at last!" he announced. "Tucker's been

picked up. They're holding him at Lemon Street station, in Soho, on a loitering with intent charge. Can you come up immediately? We'd like a statement out of him if we can get it."

"I'm on my way," said Rudd, with a sense of relief that the waiting was over and something was happening at last.

13

Bibby Tucker, who was sitting in a small, shabby interview room, looked up with a pleased expression when he saw Rudd enter.

"Oh, it's you, Mr. Rudd!" he exclaimed, sounding relieved. "I knew you'd stand by me. You'll put in a good word, won't you? You've always been fair. You tell them it's all a mistake. I wasn't trying the handles of them parked cars, honest I wasn't. You know me."

"Yes," said Rudd, sitting down on the chair opposite him, "I know you, Mr. Tucker."

He took out a packet of cigarettes, looking Tucker over as he offered it across the table. Even in the short time since he had last seen him, he noticed a further deterioration in the man. Although he still sported the double-peaked handkerchief in his breast-pocket, his suit was crumpled and there was an air of tension about him. A small nerve at one corner of his mouth kept jumping and he put up a hand to hide it.

"I don't smoke, Mr. Rudd," he said primly.

"Sorry," said Rudd, putting the packet away. "I'd forgotten, Mr. Tucker. You don't smoke and you don't drink."

"That's right," said Tucker. He was wary now, realising from the Inspector's tone of voice that something was up.

"That's what made me suspicious," Rudd went on.

"Suspicious of what?" Tucker asked, opening his eyes wide. "Honest to God, Mr. Rudd, I've always told you the truth."

"Suspicious of that conversation you said you overheard a couple of months ago in a pub; somewhere off the Strand, wasn't it?"

147

The nerve at the side of Bibby's mouth jumped and he hastily covered it with his hand.

"I was meeting a friend," he said shrilly. "I told you that at the time."

"Won't do, Bibby," Rudd replied, more in sorrow than in anger. "I checked the dates."

"I could have got the date wrong," Bibby replied, with a flash of his former verve. "I'm very busy sometimes. My business . . ."

"Your business two months ago was confined to Parkgate prison," Rudd told him. "And you weren't released until six days before you phoned me and we met at that cafe. So why don't you come clean?"

It was said with the air of giving fatherly advice. Tucker avoided the Inspector's eyes and gazed down at the scarred top of the table.

"I don't know what you're talking about," he said sulkily.

"Ah, but I do," Rudd replied blandly. "I've got all the facts, Mr. Tucker; the little set-to at the prison in which you sprained your wrist; the week you spent in the prison hospital; the fact that another prisoner from A block was brought in, quite ill with influenza and actually delirious one night and how, afterwards, you were transferred to E block where Stoll . . ."

Tucker looked up quickly. Rudd saw that the sweat had broken out along his upper lip and his eyes had the wild and staring look of a terrified horse about to bolt.

"I swear to God . . ." he began desperately.

"Why are you frightened of Stoll?" Rudd asked him. "What did he do after you'd chatted him up and told him what you'd overheard? Threaten you with the heavy mob unless you co-operated?"

"If you promise to see me all right," Tucker said, "I'll tell you the truth about everything."

"I'm promising nothing," Rudd told him, "except this: Stoll won't lay a finger on you while I can do anything to prevent it."

Tucker's eyes searched his face, looking for confirmation.

Whatever Tucker saw in Rudd's expression seemed to convince him. Running his tongue over his lips, he said, "I'll make a statement."

Rudd signalled to the constable who had been waiting just outside the door and the man entered, producing a note-book.

"It was while I was in Parkgate," Tucker began eagerly. "I got pushed down some steps and had to go into the hospital. Eddy Lisle was brought in the following night. At the time, I didn't know who it was. It was late and they'd put screens round his bed. During the night, he kept shouting out this girl's name: Milly or Molly. You know, Mr. Rudd, like I told you in the caff? I didn't take much notice at first, except he was keeping me awake. In between, he was mumbling something else that I couldn't hear. Then he said quite loudly, 'That bloody Inspector Rudd,' if you'll pardon the language. But it was the name that made me prick me ears up. Then, like I told you before, he mumbled the words 'Essex' and 'transit,' only there was a bit more to the last word that I didn't tell you. After he said it, he shouted out something else: 'I'm not going to make it.' Then the officer on night duty came over and gave him an injection and after that he must have gone to sleep because I didn't hear any more.

"The next morning one of the other patients told me who he was: Eddy Lisle. I knew he was in for armed robbery but I didn't pay it all that much attenttion, except he was one of the more important prisoners and he'd done a bank. Afterwards, when they moved me to E block, I was chatting to one of the men about it, telling him how I knew you, and Stoll must have overheard. Later, he came up to me and wanted to know all about it. Honest to God, Mr. Rudd, I'd never spoken to him before."

He paused, flickered his eyes and added, "No, that's not quite true. I had tried chatting to him once before but he'd always given me the push-off. But this time, I swear it was him who talked to me first. He asked a lot of questions like, how well did I know you? and did I know if you'd ever been connected with the Lisle brothers' case? Then he said, when we were both out, there was something I could do for him and if I did it right he'd see I got a couple of hundred quid out of it."

"Had you any idea why Stoll was interested in the Lisle brothers?" Rudd asked.

"No, not at the time," Tucker replied. "I thought maybe Stoll had it in for them for some reason. Stoll operated in

London and Vic and Eddy were from the East End. I thought it was a bit of aggro between a couple of gangs and, honest I wasn't keen to get mixed up in it."

Rudd searched his face, wondering if he were telling the truth and decided he probably was. Although Stoll had operated as a fence in London and was likely to know the underworld gossip about the full extent of the Lisle brothers' activities and the amount of stolen property that was still unrecovered, Bibby, who worked the provinces only, was probably ignorant of it.

"But I learned a bit more later," Tucker was continuing with the bright-eyed look of a man who has decided to tell all. "I'll be quite truthful with you, Mr. Rudd. When I got out, I made a few inquiries here and there and found out about all that money and I was scared, I can tell you. Stoll had told me to get in touch with him as soon as I got out of Parkgate—he'd already been released—but I decided it was too risky. I was going to clear out but I was ill. He must have had me followed because a couple of men came around to the place and told me if I didn't do what Stoll asked, they'd do me over, so I got in touch with you."

So that explained the three days' delay between Tucker being discharged and the telephone call he made later, Rudd thought. It also explained why Stoll, perhaps knowing he couldn't rely on Tucker's co-operation, had tried finding out what he could on his own from the files at the local newspaper office.

"What did he want to do?" Rudd asked him, although he already knew the answer.

"He wanted me to see you and tell you what I'd heard, only not who the man was and where I'd overheard it. That's why I said it was in a pub. He'd worked it out that you must have been involved in some way and you'd probably go around making inquiries and he'd be able to follow you and find out who you met and where you went. Once I did that, I was to lay low for a bit and, if it all turned out right, he'd let me have the couple of hundred quid he'd promised. But I wasn't going to get in touch with him, Mr. Rudd, I swear. I was going to keep clear of him and let the money go."

That was probably a lie, Rudd decided. Tucker wasn't the type to turn away a chance of making money and, although he was clearly terrified of Stoll, he hadn't done the

obvious thing and cleared out of London. Instead he had
hung about the city, hoping eventually to pick up his takings, and had been working the parked-car racket in Soho
when he had been arrested.

"That's all I know, Mr. Rudd," he concluded.

"Thank you, Mr. Tucker," Rudd said gravely. "You've
been very helpful."

"Only too pleased," Tucker replied. "Can I go now,
Mr. Rudd?"

"I'm sorry," Rudd said. "I'm afraid it's not as simple as
that."

"But you promised . . ." Tucker protested, his elderly,
lined face crumpling up.

Rudd looked at him with some sympathy.

"I said I'd do what I could, Mr. Tucker," he told him,
"and I'll keep to that. But you'll have to stay here for the
time being."

He left the room and went in search of Monk, who was
waiting in one of the offices.

"He's coughed," Rudd announced simply.

Monk's bright little eyes were amused.

"Right!" he said briskly. "It's all ready for the off, then.
I'll get Tucker to phone Frank Lisle. We might as well
make use of him while we've got him."

"Wait a minute," said Rudd. "About that charge of loitering with intent? Do you intend making it stick?"

Monk raised his shoulders.

"It's on the report sheet. He was on the old dodge of
trying the handles of parked cars. A plain-clothes man followed him the length of Brewer Street. With his record, I
can hardly let him go. But I'll put in a good word for him,
if that's the way you want it: how he's co-operated with
the police in other inquiries, blah, blah, and he may get a
reduced sentence."

"Poor little devil!" Rudd said softly.

"Come off it!" Monk said, laughing. "Don't waste any
sympathy on him. He's old enough to know better but he
never learns. He's got a record as long as my arm. Now
about the Lisle brothers . . ."

"Yes!" asked Rudd, rousing himself from contemplation
of Bibby Tucker.

"We get Tucker to phone Frank Lisle. If everything goes
according to plan, Lisle will get in touch with Bunny,

who's somewhere abroad, but God knows where. It could
be South America for all we know. We've got Home Office
permission to have Lisle's telephones tapped, both at his
office and at home, so we'll know when he does contact
him, and we've been keeping a twenty-four-hour surveillance on him. There'll be a watch kept on the air-ports and
ports to follow Bunny Lisle in case he shows up. Our own
plans are already cut and dried. Wylie's worked those out
like a full-scale battle. There'll be two mobile headquarters,
one at Tolquay and one at Merestead, both well-hidden
and both in radio contact with the main headquarters,
which they'll set up in Boxleigh. There'll also be a couple
of launches, also in radio contact, tucked away in some
inlets along the coast. By the way, the river police have
already been busy checking on your theory and they've
found the deep-water channel. It runs between two mud-
banks and lines up with the transit points you mentioned. And I had a chat myself with the man at the boat-
builder's. He's willing to co-operate with us. You were
right, there, too. He maintains Lisle's boat and Lisle always
rings him up when it's to be taken out. Then the man
checks it, sees that there's enough fuel in it and takes it
into the main basin so that it's ready when Lisle arrives.
He's seen boxes, or crates, being taken on board, too, on
one occasion, but thought they were supplies or equipment,
so didn't pay too much attention at the time. And this may
be of use to you in your case: he recognised photographs
of all the Lisle brothers, Bunny included, although he said
he hadn't seen him around for some time, but the two who
used the boat most were Vic and Eddy. He'll get in touch
with us, by the way, when Frank Lisle wants to take the
boat out, which, with a bit of luck, should be in the next
few days. High tide'll be at the right time, just as it's getting dusk, so they'll be less likely to notice the launches. I'll
be in charge of the operations at the sea-wall. Do you want
to come in on it?"

Rudd laughed suddenly. Monk's obvious excitement and
enthusiasm were catching.

"If you can find a small space for me, yes, I'd like to be
there at the kill," he replied.

"Will do," promised Monk. "But leave any rough stuff
to my men. Some of them will be armed. You're strictly an
interested observer. All right?"

"All right," agreed Rudd. "And thanks for the information. That man's evidence may prove useful if I'm ever able to bring a charge against any of the Lisle brothers. Look, Reg, I don't want to push you when you've obviously got more than enough on your plate, but I'd like some time to go through the files you've got on them. There's a chance there may be some information in them that would be useful to me."

"A few days," said Monk, "and I promise I'll have them available, although I doubt you'll find much that's any use. It's mostly details of the raids."

"I'd like a look all the same," persisted Rudd.

"Will do," Monk promised. "And now let's get Tucker in. The phone's set up in here with a tape recorder plugged into it and a couple of extensions we can listen in on."

Tucker was brought in, looking sulky and giving Rudd a reproachful glance, but when he heard what Monk wanted him to do, he became shrilly protesting.

"I've already told Mr. Rudd I don't want nothing more to do with it," he cried.

"Listen," said Monk, softly menacing. "Don't try messing me about or I might get tough and when I do, I'm not nice to know."

His eyes were hard like two little brown shoe buttons. Rudd had seen this side of him before and, although he knew that in Tucker's case it was said more for effect than in earnest, he was still a little taken aback.

Tucker looked at Rudd and the Inspector nodded to him reassuringly.

"All right," Tucker agreed unwillingly. "But I still don't think it's fair. I've got my rights, the same as anybody else."

"Detective Chief Inspector Monk may be able to put in a good word for you if you co-operate," Rudd told him, soothing him down.

Monk instructed him in what he was to say, adding, "And see you get it right, Tucker, or I may forget I ever said anything of the sort."

Tucker wetted his lips nervously.

"Supposing he finds out it's me who's rung him?" he asked.

"There's no way he can find out," Rudd assured him.

"Oh, come on!" Monk put in impatiently. " Dial this number, Tucker, and ask to speak to Mr. Frank Lisle, like I told you."

As Tucker began to dial the number Monk had given him, Monk switched on the tape recorder and the two men picked up the extensions.

A woman answered the phone, probably a secretary.

"Could I speak to Mr. Frank Lisle?" Tucker asked, his voice high-pitched with nervousness.

"Who's calling?" the woman asked.

For a moment, Tucker panicked. It was only Monk's furious grimaces over the top of his receiver that brought him to his senses.

"It's a private matter," he said. "Tell him, a friend."

The line clicked and a man's voice spoke.

"Frank Lisle here."

"Mr. Lisle, you won't know me," Tucker said, speaking rapidly in his genteel Cockney. "But a bit of info's come my way that you might be interested in."

"Yes?" said Lisle. He sounded wary.

"I've got a few contacts with the police," Tucker continued. "I'm able to do them a bit of good now and again. Well, I know this sergeant and I hear there's a lot of interest being shown in you and your brothers."

Lisle didn't answer and Tucker hurried on.

"I wasn't able to pick up much but I gather they've been in touch with the police down in Essex, whatever that means."

Lisle still didn't reply and Tucker gave a high, giggling laugh that sounded to Rudd, listening in on the extension, on the verge of hysteria. He could see the sweat breaking out on his forehead.

"I just thought I'd let you know. You may be able to do me a bit of good sometime."

"Who are you?" Lisle asked quickly.

"Never mind the name. I'll be in touch sometime," Tucker replied and rang off, wiping his face. His hands were trembling.

"Christ!" he said softly. "I hope they never find out who it was."

Monk switched off the tape recorder and, replacing his receiver, came round the desk to slap Tucker on the back. He was all bonhomie now, his eyes sparkling.

"Good man!" he was saying. "You handled that beautifully!"

"Can I go now?" Tucker asked.

Rudd turned away, leaving Monk to deal with him. He heard Tucker's voice protesting bitterly, as Monk led him away. There was, after all, little room for sentiment in the process of justice, but Rudd couldn't help feeling that he'd betrayed the man in some way.

Monk came back shortly, looking pleased with himself.

"That's the first stage set in motion," he announced. "All we have to do is wait for Frank Lisle to make a move."

Catching sight of Rudd's expression, he added, "Don't look so serious. Tucker'll have to be held. We can't do anything else. He may go running to Frank Lisle and make a balls-up of the whole thing. But I'll see there's a good word put in for him at court."

"Thanks," said Rudd.

"Now what about your plans?" Monk went on. "You don't want to go back to that dreary hotel in Boxleigh, do you? What about staying in London? You could put up at my place."

"No, thanks all the same," Rudd replied. He had met Mrs. Monk and liked her. Guilt at imposing Miller on his own sister, even though she didn't seem to mind, made him unwilling to accept the invitation. "I'll go to an hotel."

"Use the Canterbury, then. It's near Waterloo station. The man who runs it is one of my contacts and he'll see you get my calls if you mention my name. But don't tell him anything more than you have to. He works both sides of the game and he's not to be trusted."

They walked together to the steps of the police station. The sleazy world of Soho with its strip-clubs and dirty book-shops, its pimps and tarts and derelicts lay around them. Monk's world, thought Rudd. Thank God it's not mine.

"I'll be in touch," Monk was saying and, with a brief wave of his hand, walked quickly away.

Rudd made his way to the Canterbury hotel, stopping to buy a few necessities in a chain store, having left his overnight bag at Boxleigh.

Monk's name worked like a charm at the hotel and Rudd was given a quiet room at the back while the manager, a plump, ingratiating man, promised to see that he got any calls immediately.

"I'm a close friend of Mr. Monk's," he said.

Apart from thanking him, Rudd said nothing more. He sat around the hotel lounge, as he had done at the White Hart, not daring to go far in case Monk telephoned.

The call came on the morning of the second day.

"We're on the move!" Monk informed him. "I'll pick you up in about half an hour."

Rudd packed his few belongings, paid the bill and treated himself to a beer while he waited.

A large car, without any official markings, drew into the kerb an hour later and Monk, in the back seat, smiled cheerfully as Rudd walked down the steps and got in beside him.

"Worked like a charm," he told him as the car drew away into the traffic. "Frank Lisle put through a telephone call yesterday to a Mr. David Baxter, who is living quietly in a hotel in Switzerland. 'Father's ill,' he told him. 'You'd better come home at once.' As old man Lisle's been dead for years, it was obviously a prearranged warning. Anyway, we got the Swiss police on to it and they've been keeping tabs on Bunny Lisle's movements at their end. He booked a flight by Swissair that arrived at Heathrow about an hour ago where our men picked him up and followed him. According to the latest information I've got, he was last seen getting into a taxi and heading for London; no doubt to meet up with brother Frank. And Frank made another interesting call yesterday to the man at the boatyard, asking him to get the *Mariette* ready and into the main basin by today because he and a friend wanted to put in a bit of sailing later this afternoon. So we're all set at that end as well. Our men are already moving into position."

"So it looks as if they're almost in the bag," Rudd commented.

He had caught something of Monk's excitement but only at second-hand. It wasn't his case, after all. He wasn't involved in quite the same way as Monk was.

They stopped briefly for lunch at some anonymous cafe on the arterial road out of London and were on their way again shortly afterwards.

The countryside began to be familiar to Rudd. He was on his own territory now and the names on the road-signs were ones he knew. They swept through Chelmsford and were out again on the road leading to Merestead.

On the outskirts of the village, Monk pointed to a farmhouse. "See that barn? There's a mobile headquarters hidden away behind it. Thank God the countryside's so bloody flat round here, we haven't had any trouble with radio communciation."

They parked in a secluded field near the church where several other cars were already standing.

"We're using ordinary vehicles," Monk explained as they got out. "Less suspicious but I'll have a Panda car and some foot patrols posted in the village later when things really get moving. I don't want any of the locals traipsing across the fields for a look-see. Frank and Bunny may be armed. Some of my men are carrying guns, just in case they do try shooting their way out. Three of them are crack shots with rifles."

He looked up at the sky and added:

"Thank Christ it isn't raining."

It was the first time Rudd had noticed the weather. The two days spent in London had broken his contact with the elements. Unless it were actually raining or snowing, you hardly noticed what was going on above the roof-tops.

It was a day of thin sunshine and small breezes that riffled the grass, turning every blade glossy. In the lane that led past Thorpe's old cottage, the hawthorn buds were beginning to break on the hedges.

He passed the cottage this time without a pang. The presence of Monk and the others who had come with them in the car, an inspector called Tiler and a sergeant who had acted as driver, had destroyed the spell the place had for him.

As they walked across the field towards the sea-wall, Rudd could see the men were already in position, about twenty of them, some in uniform, some in plain-clothes. Three rifles lay propped against the bank of the dyke while, nearby, a man was crouching over a radio receiver, checking the signal.

Apart from this activity, nothing much seemed to be happening. The men were relaxed, lying and sitting on the grass, smoking and talking. It was not yet time for the action to begin.

Monk scrambled up the sea-wall, propping his elbows on the top of it and using the binoculars he had hanging by a strap round his neck to survey the terrain. Rudd joined him.

"There's one launch tucked away to the right," Monk told him, waving an arm. "It's well-hidden. The other's down the coast, between here and Tolquay. There're no other boats about, thank God. I don't want Frank Lisle frightened off at the last minute. And the sea's calm. They shouldn't have any difficulty getting in through that channel. Harvey's picked a perfect day for it. He was worrying over the weather forecasts this morning like a bride."

Rudd looked out across the marshes. It was, as Monk said, a perfect day. The sunlight glittered on the wide stretches of water, turning them to sheets of moving silver. Below him, in the creek, the tide was running back, covering the shining mud and the long rectangle of the lighter, its rim draped with weed that the water was beginning to float away.

"Could I borrow the glasses for a minute?" he asked Monk.

Adjusting the focus, Rudd trained them on the far stretch of marsh on the other side of the village. Thorpe's house-boat jumped out at him with its crazy superstructure and iron stovepipe trickling smoke. A small white speck lying on the deck he took to be the dog. He remembered Thorpe's terrible eagerness, his hands clutching into fists. With any luck, he'd soon be able to appease it.

"Thanks," he said to Monk, handing his glasses back.

"Seen all you want to?" Monk asked him.

"Yes," Rudd replied.

Monk glanced at his watch.

"We shouldn't have long to wait now," Monk said. "Another hour and the tide should be high. Let's get back down and sort the men out."

They slithered down the bank just as the man on the radio receiver raised a hand to call him over.

"It's headquarters, sir. One of the patrol cars has reported Lisle's car has just turned off the main road and is heading for Tolquay."

"Right!" said Monk, snapping into immediate activity.

"I want you men in position. You can continue smoking and talking but I want silence and fags out the minute I give the command. Understand?"

The men moved out along the bottom of the sea-wall, sitting propped up against its slope. There was very little conversation, despite what Monk had said. The men with the rifles checked them over while Monk went to squat beside the radio receiver.

A half hour passed and, in that time, the light began imperceptibly to fade, the sky turning from pale blue to darker blue and then to a tender purple as the dusk drew in. Then suddenly, Monk was on his feet, moving along the line of men.

"They're on their way. They're moving out of the basin. Fags out and if any man so much as breathes heavily in the next half hour, I'll do for him personally. No-one's to fire unless I give the word. Is that understood?"

A low murmur of assent spread through the line and died. The men had turned now to face the bank, lying spread-eagled against it. Rudd lay with them. Although he was to play no active part, he felt the tension and excitement mounting in himself. The silence was almost palpable, like a dome arching over them so that all sound seemed strangely remote, part of another world. On the far side of the dyke, Rudd could hear water lapping as the tide ran in and the cry of a sea-bird, immeasurably forlorn.

Presently, far off to their left, they heard another sound, the put-putter of a boat's engine that grew steadily louder.

14

It was approaching from their left, moving towards them out of sight behind the bank of the sea-wall. Rudd turned his head, following its progress. It was now the only sound audible. The cry of the bird and the steady lapping of the water were lost in it. He was no longer even aware of the other men. All his attention was concentrated into the act of listening.

Presently the engine was throttled down and men's voices could be heard carrying clearly over the water.

"Bunny! Are they in line yet?"

It was the voice that Rudd had heard speaking on the telephone at Lemon Street police station to Bibby Tucker: Frank Lisles's.

A younger, lighter voice answered him, urgent with tension.

"Wait! Wait! *Now!*"

The engine picked up again for a few seconds and then its note died down once more.

Although he could hear nothing, Rudd could imagine the scene that was taking place on the far side of the dyke. The boat was idling gently as it nosed its way into the deep-water channel through the mud-banks.

"Steady! Keep her steady, for Christ's sake!" It was Bunny Lisle's voice again. Then he said, less urgently, "Ease her down while I put in the markers."

He would be standing, Rudd imagined, on the fore-deck, in front of the cabin, the poles ready to be thrust into the mud-banks on either side as they drifted past the exit of the channel into the wider stretch of deep water at the opening of the creek.

"Right!" Bunny Lisle was saying. His voice sounded more relaxed. They must be safely through.

Once again, the engine picked up power. They would be turning now, in readiness to approach the lighter stern first. Then the engine was cut altogether and nothing was heard for a few seconds except the slap of water and the sound of feet on the wooden deck.

Then Frank Lisle spoke.

"Are you ready up your end, Bunny? Then push!"

The voice sounded startlingly near. Rudd, tensed up with listening and waiting, felt the muscles in the back of his neck stiffen as he heard it. Beside him, Monk, who was spread-eagled against the bank, like a soldier in a trench waiting to go over the top, turned his head with exquisite care to look along the line of men. The barrels of the rifles were slanting upwards, held slightly away from the slope of the bank so as not to impede the men when the order came for them to move forward.

Catching Rudd's glance, Monk grinned broadly and winked. His face was luminous and Rudd realised he was laughing silently, inside himself, as jubilant as a small boy on a long-awaited treat.

A few feet away from them, on the other side of the bank, Frank and Bunny Lisle were poling the boat along the side of the bank. They could hear them grunting with the effort, the gurgle of the water as the boat moved forward and the dull thud of the poles as they were thrust into the slope.

Rudd, lying against the wall with his face pressed against the grass, fancied he could feel as well as hear the impact. The earth seemed to vibrate with the force of each thrust.

Frank Lisle spoke again. He was out of breath, struggling to get the words out.

"Okay, Bunny. Tie her your end. Don't let her drift."

Bunny's voice answered.

"All right. I know what to do. Don't fuss, Frank. And for God's sake, sit down for a moment."

"We haven't got time. The light's going."

"Then take it easy."

"Is she moored properly your end?"

"Yes!"

Bunny sounded impatient. He seemed to resent Frank's assumption of authority. Perhaps, having broken away to some extent from the family circle, unlike Vic and Eddy, he was less willing to accept orders from his eldest brother.

"I'll get the winch ready," Frank was saying. "Take one of the poles and see if you can feel any of the boxes. Vic said he put them in close together up this end of the lighter but they'll be under the mud by now."

Footsteps again sounded on the decking and then the splash and gurgle of water as Bunny Lisle probed the mud.

"I think I've found some of them!" he announced excitedly after a few minutes. "They're not too deep in either. It shouldn't be difficult getting them out."

"How many?" Frank Lisle asked.

"Five, I think."

"Christ! There should be seven!"

Bunny laughed.

"They're all down there somewhere. It's not likely anyone's stolen them."

"All right! You can cut out the funny stuff." Frank Lisle sounded annoyed. "The winch is ready. I'll start the engine up in a moment. Now, listen, Bunny, the idea is to lower the hook slowly; get it fixed firmly in the chains before we start lifting . . ."

"I know, I know. You've told me at least three times already."

"Then get it right!" Frank Lisle snapped. "We don't want to still be here when it's dark. I'll get the engine started."

Feet moved along the deck and shortly afterwards the engine sputtered into life, drowning their voices.

Rudd, who had been listening with such complete absorption that he had forgotten his immediate surroundings, was aware that, beside him, Monk was lifting his hand.

The men, who had been lying motionless, began inching their way slowly up the bank, Monk with them, using his elbows to propel himself upwards. A few inches from the top, they halted; Monk again looking along the line of men as they straddled the slope, their legs spread wide to keep a purchase on the bank, their heads tucked down so that they would be out of sight above the sea-wall.

The boat's engine droned on. Time seemed suspended. Rudd was acutely aware now of his surroundings; of the sky overhead, purpling into dusk; of the smell of grass and the feel of it, cool and slippery, under his hands. Above him, a flock of small birds darted away, making for home.

At the same time, as if it were a signal, Monk again raised his arm. The next second, the men had flung themselves forward and upward so that they were now lying belly down on the path that ran along the top of the seawall and Monk was shouting:

"All right, Lisle! Get your hands up! You're both covered."

The subsequent moments were full of noise and activity. There were shouts, Monk calling out orders, men moving quickly into their prearranged positions. The three armed policemen stood upright on the top of the wall, keeping their guns trained downwards on the scene that was going on beyond Rudd's line of vision on the far side of the bank. Monk, together with most of the men, had disappeared out of sight. As a background to it all, the engine of the boat went on running.

Suddenly it was cut. In the ensuing silence, other sounds were becoming audible, feet moving and scuffling, a voice swearing loudly and obscenely. Then Monk's, raised above it.

"I said, get moving, Lisle!"

The armed men on top of the dyke tensed, as if expecting trouble. But whatever crisis was happening, it must have passed over, because shortly afterwards several policemen came scrambling over the top of the sea-wall, positioning themselves on the top of it and down its side to form a cordon through which two men were hustled.

Rudd watched them with undisguised interest. They were both wearing sailing clothes, yellow waterproof trousers and jackets and they slithered awkwardly down the slope, handcuffed by each wrist to uniformed policemen who were also finding it difficult to keep their balance on the damp grass.

Although Rudd had never seen the Lisle brothers, it was easy to distinguish between them from the information Monk had already given him. Frank Lisle was in his forties, tall and broad-shouldered, full-faced and good-looking, with thick fair hair that was beginning to turn grey. Bunny was younger, more slightly built, but fair-haired like Frank.

Both men's reactions showed clearly in their faces. Frank Lisle was furiously angry. Although restrained by the policemen to whom he was handcuffed, he was ready to break free, his massive shoulders hunched, his head lowered between them. He reminded Rudd of a bull straining to break its chain.

Bunny Lisle was too frightened to put up any resistance. He seemed to flinch away as Monk went over to speak to him, but when Monk moved off, he had sufficiently recovered for his face to assume a sulky look.

Perhaps it was why Frank Lisle had used him in only the one hold-up, knowing he lacked the aggression and toughness to carry through the other raids. Of one thing Rudd was sure at this first encounter with him, it was unlikely Bunny Lisle had murdered Melanie Thorpe. He would kill only on an impulse. Of Frank Lisle he was not so positive. The man looked ruthless enough to carry out any act of violence. But his money was still on the other two brothers he had not yet seen. Vic and Eddy. From the little he had overheard on board the boat that evening, it seemed to him more likely than ever that it was Vic and Eddy who had been responsible for placing the boxes in the lighter and, therefore, had almost certainly been present on that Sunday afternoon four years before.

Monk was moving about, giving quiet orders, completely in charge. The man at the radio was sending out a message to the mobile headquarters outside the village and Monk went over to speak to someone himself. Presently, he joined Rudd.

"The van's coming," he told him. "It'll park at the top of the lane. I'll get these two villains on their way."

He spoke to a uniformed inspector and the group of men surrounding the Lisle brothers began moving off across the field, Bunny and Frank still flanked by the constables to whom they were handcuffed.

Monk watched them go with a satisfied look on his face.

"It does your heart good," he said softly, almost to himself.

The radio operator was calling to attract his attention.

"The launches are waiting to move into position, sir."

"Tell them they can get started," Monk replied. To Rudd, he added, "Want to see it? It's the last act in this particular bit of the drama."

They climbed to the top of the sea-wall, Rudd moving a

little clumsily at first. The long wait in the damp grass had stiffened his muscles.

At the top, he looked about him. Twilight was dropping swiftly now over the marshes. Out to sea it was no longer possible to tell where the water ended and the sky began. Both were the same colour of dusk. Inland, the marshes were still just visible, with small glints of silver where the last light caught the water in the creeks and inlets. Immediately below him, the *Mariette* was moored, stern first, tied fore and aft to the stakes in the bank. Two boat poles lay abandoned on the deck. The other two were sticking out of the water further off, near the opening of the creek.

As he watched, he saw a launch approaching from the right, speeding along the coast, then circling and drifting towards the shore, its engine idling.

"The light's nearly gone," Monk remarked. "They'll have lost the transit points but the boat poles will act as markers."

As the launch approached, he noticed for the first time how close together they were. The unseen channel would be only just wide enough to take a boat, with very little room to spare. No wonder Eddy Lisle had shouted "I'm not going to make it!" in his delirium. Getting a boat through it would be a tricky undertaking. It could easily finish up stranded on the banks.

The launch made it, easing its way through, and then the engine note increased in power as the boat made a tight circle and began approaching the creek stern first. The engine was cut and two men with poles began pushing the launch up the creek. They hadn't far to take it. The *Mariette* already took up several feet of the bank. Inch by inch they thrust it through the water until the stern of the launch was almost touching the prow of the cruiser and then a man jumped across the intervening gap and secured ropes to the *Mariette* and to the nearest mooring stake. He was joined by others from the police launch, two in frogmen's suits. On board the launch, someone switched on a powerful light on the roof of the wheelhouse and in its brilliant beam Monk and Rudd watched the activities of the men ten feet below them. It was then Rudd noticed a second launch standing out to sea not far from the creek entrance, waiting in case it was needed.

The frog-men lowered themselves into the water over the stern of the *Mariette* and for several minutes neither of them was visible. Then one bobbed up, gave a thumbs-up signal and the engine of the *Mariette* was started up. The barrel of the winch began to revolve, the hawser tightened and ran backwards and the hook on the end of it descended into the water, the frog-men guiding it and disappearing with it under the surface. Shortly afterwards the two men reappeared, the winch began to run in reverse and the hook emerged from the water, a steel box bound with chains into which it was fastened dangling at the end of it and dripping muddy water and sea-weed. The men on the *Mariette* hauled it aboard.

"Jackpot!" said Monk jubilantly and shouted down to the men, "There should be six more like it down there!"

"We've located them, sir!" one of the men shouted back.

They watched in the gathering dusk until all the seven boxes were safely on board and the men were preparing to leave. Then Monk turned to Rudd.

"Ready?" he asked. "There's nothing more we can do here. They'll take the *Mariette* back to London, together with the loot. Mace is in charge of it that end. I'll follow Frank and Bunny by road to London. They should be well on their way now. Can I drop you off at Chelmsford?"

"Can you make it Boxleigh?" Rudd replied. "I've got to pick up my car and bag from the White Hart."

"Will do," said Monk.

They walked back towards the village.

"Well, that's my case closed," said Monk. He sounded well pleased with himself.

"But not mine," Rudd reminded him.

Monk gave him a quick, appraising look.

"You still think it's one of the Lisle brothers?"

"I'm convinced of it in my own mind."

"But which one?"

"Not Frank or Bunny, of that I'm sure now. Do you remember we heard Frank say Vic had put the boxes in the near end of the lighter? I think it was Vic and Eddy who were responsible for disposing of the loot. They'd have more chance, too, of taking a day off and coming down to Tolquay without it looking suspicious. From what you told me, they were in the habit of shutting up their work-shop when business was slack and taking a market stall somewhere. It'd make an excellent alibi for any trips out of London. Frank and Bunny with their closer business ties wouldn't have found it so easy to get away."

"That's true," Monk agreed and added thoughtfully, "Vic or Eddy. The point is, which one?"

"I don't know," confessed Rudd. "It could be either. If I'm right, there were two of them in the car with her, one driving and one in the back who leaned forward and strangled her. If we're to believe Tucker and I think we must—after all, I've only got this far in the case by accepting that what he told me was largely correct—then it was Eddy Lisle who shouted out her name, but that doesn't necessarily mean he killed her. He may have only witnessed it. The trouble is, Reg, they're too shadowy as figures. I can't picture them as individuals. That's the main reason I want to go through the files at the Yard. There may be something, a tiny detail even, that could give me a hint."

"You're not hoping for positive evidence, then?" Monk asked.

"At this late stage?" Rudd replied. "It'd be a miracle."

"Well, I said I'd do what I could," Monk said, "and I'll keep to it. If you care to come up to the Yard tomorrow, I'll see that the files are available for you to go through. And I'll try to turn up some gossip about them that might be useful. As I told you, I never met either of them. They were two men we sent down on an armed robbery charge, that's about as much as I know. Anyway, it was Frank Lisle I was most interested in. I saw him as the brains behind the operations."

They came to the centre of the village, almost deserted now except for a Panda car still in position. Monk went over to speak to the driver and the car drove off.

"What about Stoll?" he asked Rudd as they took the road out of the village. "If there's any justice we ought to be able to round him up as well. Complete the bag, so to speak. But I can't see any charge we can bring against him. Following you around was hardly breaking the law."

Rudd smiled to himself in the darkness of the car and settled himself back comfortably in his seat.

"I've got something lined up for him," he replied, "and, as you said, if there's any justice, we'll pull him in, too."

Monk gave him an amused look.

"I wish you luck," he said.

At Boxleigh, he dropped Rudd off outside the hotel, where Rudd retrieved his overnight bag, paid his bill and, collecting Miller's car, set off on the road back to Chelmsford, stopping at the first public telephone on the way to put through a call to Superintendent Davies at headquarters.

"I'm on my way, sir," he informed him. "The Lisle brothers have been arrested. Any joy with that inquiry?"

"Yes," Davies told him. "Your hunch was correct. Do you want to make the arrest yourself?"

"I'd like to," Rudd replied. After all, the man had followed him about for three days, forcing him to abandon his comfortable home for the dreary lounge and indifferent cooking of the White Hart. It seemed only a fair retribution.

"Could you let Sergeant Boyce know I'm on my way and we'll pick Stoll up?"

"Won't Stoll notice you arriving and get suspicious?" Davies asked. "He may clear off and then where'll you be?"

"I don't think that's likely," Rudd replied. "I'm driving Miller's car and if Stoll's parked where he usually is, in that cul-de-sac, he won't be able to see who's behind the wheel. I'll slip in by the back entrance."

"Right," said Davies. "I'll see Boyce gets your message."

He rang off and Rudd completed the journey back to headquarters, where he left the car near the rear doors and ducked quickly inside the building. Boyce was waiting for him in his office, pleased at the prospect of arresting Stoll as if he'd been personally vindicated.

"And about time, too," he commented.

"We'll take Miller with us," Rudd said. "Minus his wig. I think he deserves to be in on this as well. And who's good with a car? The street where he's parked is a dead-end so he can't get out at the top. But he may try a quick get-away, especially if he sees me coming and realises something's up."

"Jackson?" suggested Boyce.

"Right, Jackson it is. Tell him to take one of the vans and park near the end of the road, but keeping well back out of sight until we're ready to move in."

Boyce went off to pass on the instructions to Jackson,

returning to the office with Miller. Rudd looked him up and down with amusement.

"I hear Stoll was getting you down," he remarked.

Miller grinned.

"It was a bit tantalising, sir. I had to keep controlling this urge to shake him off and lose him."

"I know the feeling," Rudd sympathised. "I hope you were comfortable at my sister's?"

"Oh, yes, very," Miller said promptly and added, "She's a very good cook."

"Yes, she is," Rudd agreed. Turning to Boyce, he said, "Jackson ought to be in position by now. Are you ready?"

They left the building separately, Miller and Boyce by the back, Rudd by the front. As he had resumed his own identity, there was no reason why Stoll should be suspicious of his presence. He walked along on the right, as if making for the car-park. Ahead of him, Miller and Boyce crossed the road. Jackson, in the van with the engine ticking over, was parked a little in front of the entrance of the cul-de-sac, ready to move forward and block the street.

At the last moment, Rudd crossed the road. Boyce and Miller were already nearly level with Stoll's car, a small grey Austin this time. Stoll saw Rudd coming but his attention was diverted at the last moment by Boyce tapping on the driver's window as Miller closed in on the passenger's side. His hand was on the ignition key but he was too late. Before he had time to switch on the engine, Rudd was at Boyce's side, leaning in at the window to say pleasantly:

"Good evening, Mr. Stoll."

Stoll's pallid face looked up at him.

"Do I know you?" he asked.

It was, Rudd thought, not a bad attempt at brazening it out.

"You ought to, Mr. Stoll. You've been following me around for long enough. But it's been a bit of a wasted effort, I'm afraid. We picked the Lisle brothers up tonight, together with the loot. Quite a nice little tidy sum it was, too."

Stoll ran his tongue over his lips, looking from Rudd, with Boyce's bulky figure looming behind him, to Miller, guarding the door on the passenger's side.

"I don't know what you're on about," he said contemptuously. "I'm waiting for a friend."

"Mr. Beeson, or his son?" Rudd asked. "I shouldn't bother waiting for either of them if I were you. You'll be meeting them later at the station when we bring them in."

"You're arresting me?" Stoll asked. He sounded incredulous. "On what grounds? You've got nothing on me."

"Oh, yes, we have," Rudd replied regretfully. "The car you're driving is stolen. The owner missed it from the carpark of the Red Dragon at Lamstead two nights ago. I'm afraid the Beesons have been a bit overzealous in their effort to provide you with a different car every day, Mr. Stoll. They're small, greedy men, and they couldn't turn down a chance of making money, so when they ran out of legitimate cars, I'm sorry to say they turned their hands to knocking them off. So, if you'll hand over the keys and accompany me to headquarters. . . ."

Stoll swore long and fluently as he got out of the car.

"Tchk! Tchk!" said Boyce disapprovingly as he moved in. What happened next was totally unexpected. Whether Stoll panicked at the prospect of a further prison sentence or whether the time spent in tailing Rudd had stretched his own nerves to breaking point, the Inspector could only guess. But Boyce's hand placed on his arm triggered off a violent reaction. Stoll took a wild swing at the Sergeant, knocking him off balance, and sprinted for the end of the street. He did not get very far. Miller ran after him, and Boyce, quickly recovering, also set off in pursuit while Jackson, who had driven the van across the entrance, jumped out and closed in on him from the front. There was a brief scuffle in which Stoll was quickly overcome.

Rudd strolled up.

"That was a stupid thing to do, Mr. Stoll," he remarked mildly. "It'll all have to go down on the charge sheet, you know. Resisting arrest. Assaulting a police officer. It won't look too good with your previous record, will it?"

Unlike Tucker's case, he felt no regrets as Stoll was later taken away to the cells. The man's personality had lain like a shadow over the investigation, oddly disquieting, and Rudd was more than glad to see the back of him. That part of the case, at least, was satisfactorily closed.

There remained, however, the main inquiry into the murder of Melanie Thorpe, and the next morning, after a comfortable night spent in his own bed, Rudd set off for the Yard.

Monk was as good as his word and had seen to it that a small office had been set aside for the Inspector's use and it was in here that the files on the Lisle brothers had been placed in two great stacks on the floor.

Rudd looked at them disconsolately as he was shown into the room. If there was anything of use to him in his inquiry, it would be there, in that mass of papers.

The files were in chronological order, starting with the first raid on the jeweller's shop in Beckenham ten years before. Carrying it over to the desk, he sat down and, opening it, began to read.

He continued reading all the rest of that day, with only a short break for lunch, working his way through the stacks of files. The evidence in them was full and detailed: witnesses' accounts of the various raids, reports on the stolen cars, lists of the stolen property, but, at the end of the day, he had found nothing that seemed of use to him in his own inquiries. The figures remained shadowy and anonymous, men in goggles and helmets, indistinguishable from each other except for their build, although it seemed likely, as Monk had pointed out, that Frank Lisle had played the part of the well-to-do customer on the jewellers' hold-ups. But, in the statements covering the bank-raids, in which Vic and Eddy, presumably, had acted as security men, Rudd could see that the uniforms had given them not only a convenient disguise but also a psychological cover. In adopting the clothing, they seemed also to have assumed a certain manner of behaving that was identical. Again and again, as he read through the reports, he was struck by the interchangeability of their roles. In one raid, it was the taller of the two who had held the other customers at gun-point. In another, the more slightly built of the two men had performed the same action.

Monk had said they were a pair. Born close together, with less than a year between them, they had shared a flat and together ran a business, taking time off now and again to return to their old family tradition of street-trading. Of Eddy, he knew a little more. He had been married and divorced. In hospital he had been ill and had never fully recovered. Of Vic, he knew even less. And the reports added nothing to the little he knew. They emerged as two menacing figures, one taller than the other, and that was all.

And nowhere, in all that mass of paper, was Rudd able to find any detail, however small, that linked them with the Melanie Thorpe murder.

At five o'clock he gave up and went home, returning the following morning to set to work reading the remaining files: those dealing with the more recent raids on the bullion and diamond dealers.

He was halfway through them when Monk, carrying yet another file, came into the office to find Rudd humped dispiritedly over the typewritten pages of a witness's statement.

"Any luck?" he asked.

Rudd looked up.

"Nothing so far," he admitted. "It's all good official stuff that tells me damn all about them as personalities. Were you able to find out anything by asking around?"

"Not much," Monk replied. "A few bits and pieces here and there. I'll tell you in a minute. Meanwhile, I'm sending out for coffee. You look in need of a break."

Going to the door, he shouted to some unseen constable, "Fetch us a couple of coffees, Stewart, and some biscuits."

Closing the door, he added, "I've brought you this. The last file on them, when they were nabbed on the final bank-raid. I thought you might like to have a look at their mug-shots."

Turning to the relevant pages, he handed the file over to Rudd. The photographs were stapled to a sheet of paper that also listed other details about them, their age, weight, height and colouring.

For the first time, Rudd found himself looking at the faces of the two men, one of whom might be the killer of Melanie Thorpe.

Eddy Lisle bore a marked resemblance to his brother Frank. He had the same good-looking, full face with thick, springy fair hair. The neck above the shirt collar was strong and, although the photograph stopped short at the shoulders, it was possible to guess the man's powerful physique. He'd be physically capable, Rudd thought, of strangling a girl quickly and efficiently, before she had time to put up a struggle.

Otherwise, the photographs told him little. The flashlight by which they had been taken, while showing the features in good detail, had given them a flat, shadowless appearance, without subtlety of expression. The one in profile was no better. The nose was thicker and coarser than the full-face picture had suggested, the chin a little heavier, with a fold of flesh already beginning to form under it, indicating that, as he grew older, he would probably put on weight. But there was nothing in either photograph of Eddy Lisle to indicate any special quality of character that might suggest a killer.

He glanced across the page to the photographs of Vic Lisle and was struck, first of all, by the lack of any physical similarity to any of his brothers, although, like Bunny, he seemed slighter built. But while Bunny was fair and boyish in appearance, Vic had a dark, narrow face with a sharp V-shaped frown mark between his eyebrows and a long chin that gave an odd, heavy-bottomed look to his face. There was more personality showing in his photographs than in Eddy's. Rudd could guess at something of his character: hard, suspicious, tough. But did that necessarily make him a murderer?

A knock came at the door at this point and a constable entered carrying a tray on which were two cups of coffee and a plate containing four biscuits.

After he had gone, Monk said, "I gather from the look on your face that the photographs haven't helped all that much."

"At least I know what they look like now," Rudd replied. "But, apart from that, I'm no further forward. As far as I'm concerned, it could still be either of them. What were you able to find out?"

"As I said, not a lot. As both men carried guns, they were presumably both prepared to use them, so that doesn't give us much to go on. When they were charged, Vic had nothing to say at all. Just sat there with his arms folded and wouldn't open his mouth. Eddy seemed more nervous, kept running his hand over his hair. Later, they both made statements. They're there in the file I've just given you. One bit of gossip may be relevant, although I doubt it. Frank's solicitor handled Eddy's divorce for him, but we might have guessed that already. Frank liked to play big brother."

As Monk was speaking, Rudd was turning the pages of the file that Monk had placed on the desk, looking for the statements the men had made when they were charged.

Monk watched him with sympathy.

"I don't know what you're hoping to find," he said, "and I don't want to rush you, but the top men will want to have all this lot back in circulation fairly soon. They're listing the stuff we found in the lighter at the moment but they'll need the files to start building up the charge sheet."

"All right," Rudd replied. "I understand, Reg. Let me just have a quick look through this one and then I'll call it a day."

He turned a page and then stopped suddenly, staring at the single sheet in front of him.

"Reg," he said softly, "do you believe in Fate? Because I think I do."

Leaning swiftly across the table, he picked up the telephone and, dialling the number of Parkgate prison, asked to speak to the Governor.

Monk, who had stretched across for the sheet of paper, began reading it as Rudd spoke to McKinley. He raised his eyebrows as Rudd rang off, his request made.

"Something in this?" he asked incredulously.

"Yes," replied Rudd quietly, "and something so small and trivial I might have overlooked it. Do you want to come with me, Reg? Be in at my kill?"

They drove through the London mid-day rush-hour and it was only on the northern outskirts of the city that they were able to pick up any speed. As they drove, Rudd explained the significance of what he had discovered.

McKinley welcomed them into his office and, after Rudd had introduced Monk to him, the Governor indicated his desk, on which two large, brown envelopes were lying.

"I've sent for their possessions as you asked," he said. "We've been holding them here. There's not much in them as you can see for yourself."

He tipped the contents of the first envelope onto the top of the desk.

"Vic Lisle's," he said.

Rudd glanced at them quickly. There was a wrist-watch, a wallet, some loose change and a bunch of keys. Vic Lisle evidently hadn't been carrying much on him the day he was arrested.

"And Eddy's?" asked Rudd.

The second envelope contained more. As McKinley

emptied it, the contents came out slowly onto the sheet of blotting paper which he had spread to receive them. There was a wallet, too, and a watch, a heavy signet ring, a St. Christopher medallion on a silver chain and a small leather folder that seemed to contain photographs and letters. The final object had to be shaken out as it had caught itself in the flap of the envelope. At last, it came free and fell onto the blotter, bouncing and rolling a little distance away from the other things. It was a little plastic key-ring in the shape of a black cat with green glass eyes.

Rudd stood looking down on it without touching it. It was Monk who spoke.

"Eureka!" he said joyfully.

McKinley looked from one to the other of them a little puzzled.

"I'm not sure what you've found," he began.

"The identity of a girl's murderer," Rudd replied. Picking up the cat, he ran his fingers over its crude, mass-produced shape.

"I'd like an interview with Eddy Lisle," he told McKinley.

15

They were taken to a small room where, after a few minutes' delay, Eddy Lisle was brought in, accompanied by a warder.

As he entered, Rudd looked at him with a quick, searching glance. Although he had seen only photographs of him before he was shocked by the change in the man's appearance. The flesh of his full, good-looking face had fallen away, revealing the heavy, bony structure beneath. His hair, too, had thinned and receded and was turning grey. He walked with a stooping gait and yet it was possible to see, even in the physical wreck he had become, the former strong physique and powerful shoulders. Beside him, he heard Monk give an involuntary sharp intake of breath.

"Sit down, Mr. Lisle," Rudd said pleasantly. The man seated himself awkwardly on the chair that had been set ready for him on the opposite side of the table. "This is Detective Chief Inspector Monk of Scotland Yard and I'm Detective Inspector Rudd of the Essex police."

For a moment, the name seemed to mean nothing to Lisle. His face remained blank, and then, suddenly, as he became aware of Rudd's identity, his expression changed to one of alarm.

"I think you already know who I am," Rudd said, "and why I'm here."

Lisle recovered quickly. His face closed over and he assumed a sullen look.

He shook his head.

"Melanie Thorpe?" suggested Rudd.

"Who's she? Never heard of her," Lisle replied quickly.

"The girl at Merestead?" Rudd prompted him.

Eddy shrugged and didn't reply. Rudd searched his face, looking for a hint in its expression as to how he might best proceed. Although he held the trump card, he was anxious not to play it too soon.

"You were heard calling out her name when you were ill in the prison hospital," Rudd pointed out.

This piece of information clearly disturbed him but he was quick to cover it up.

"Did I? That don't mean nothing. I once went out with a girl called Melanie. Melanie Hunt. You can ask anybody. Her dad kept a pub in the Walworth Road."

It was then that a look came into Lisle's face that gave the Inspector the first indication of weakness in the man that he could exploit to his own advantage.

"You've had quite a few girl-friends in your time, haven't you, Mr. Lisle?" he asked in a conversational voice.

The unexpected question caught Lisle off guard. He looked surprised but also gratified.

"Come on," coaxed Rudd. "There's nothing to be ashamed of. You're a good-looking man, after all."

Eddy Lisle passed a hand over his hair; a gesture this time not of nervousness but of physical reassurance.

Beside the Inspector, Monk looked quickly down at his own hands. He had seen various interviewing techniques before but never this subtle, almost cruel yet friendly-seeming approach. Rudd's face reflected a warm, open expression that contrasted sharply with the ruined looks of the man sitting opposite him.

"I've had a few girl-friends in my time," Lisle replied, trying to appear off-hand.

"So you chatted her up?" Rudd went on easily, as if it followed naturally on what had already been said.

It took Eddy Lisle a moment to realise what was happening. Then his face went blank.

"Who?" he asked.

"Melanie Thorpe," Rudd replied promptly. "You know, the girl who came walking along the sea-wall that Sunday afternoon, the day you and Vic were putting the boxes into the lighter."

Eddy started to say something but Rudd ignored him, carrying on with his story in a slightly bored voice as if he already knew it too well.

"She had a little white mongrel dog with her. Not a very

pretty girl, I'll admit. Not really your type at all. But you have this knack with women, so you chatted her up and later you offered her a lift home from the bus stop. Poor kid! She didn't get very far along the road before you pulled in at a gate opening and strangled her."

"It's a lie!" Eddy cried hoarsely. "You're trying to put one over on me. I've told you I don't know nothing about this girl."

Rudd didn't answer but, reaching into his pocket, he took out the little black cat key-ring, which he placed on the table.

"Yours, I think?" he said. "At least, it was found on you the day you were arrested."

Eddy Lisle looked down at it. Whether or not he recognised it, it was impossible to tell.

"Yours?" asked Rudd again.

"I don't know," Eddy said after a pause. "Are you sure it's not Vic's?"

"Oh, no, not Vic's!" said Rudd with complete confidence. "Vic's not like that. You're the sentimental one, Eddy; the one who wears a St. Christopher medallion and carries a wallet full of photographs and old letters when he goes on a bank-raid. Vic's the sort who keeps his possessions down to a minimum. Vic . . ."

A spasm of rage passed over Eddy Lisle's face.

"For Christ's sake," he shouted, "don't bloody keep on about Vic!"

And it was then that Rudd finally understood.

"Frank and Vic," he said softly. "Not you and Vic, after all. That's the way it was, wasn't it, Eddy? Frank as top dog, giving orders, then Vic next in line, giving his. With you at the bottom of the heap, taking it from both of them. Bunny should have been last but he had the sense to clear out. You tried once, though, didn't you? You got married. But it didn't last long. Frank fixed up for your divorce and you were back again, under their thumbs. Who was it told you to kill her? Vic?"

"No!" shouted Eddy. "I swear to God!"

"Then it was Vic who did it," Rudd said, as if he'd known it all along. "You drove and he sat in the back. Wasn't that how it was, Eddy?"

"He said . . ."

"Chat her up?" Rudd suggested.

"Oh, Christ, if I'd only known," Eddy cried.

"She came walking along the sea-wall," Rudd repeated. The words seemed to mesmerise Eddy. "With the little white dog at her heels . . ."

"We didn't hear her coming," Eddy Lisle said. He seemed too exhausted to hold out any longer. "The first thing we knew, she was there on the top, watching us. I smiled and said 'Good afternoon' to her. Then she asked us what we were doing. Vic said we were trying a bit of salvaging but she didn't seem to believe us. She said, 'You won't find much there. It's an old lighter. You'd do better out in the channel.' It was then Vic told me to talk to her, find out who she was. He kept nudging and whispering. He said, 'She knows too much. She might let on what she's seen.' "

"So you chatted to her?" Rudd said encouragingly.

Eddy Lisle nodded. He seemed almost relieved now to tell his version.

"I got out on the bank and joined her, talked about the dog, at first. Then the boat. She seemed to like it. I said maybe we could take her out for a trip in it one day. She said yes, she'd like that. So I said, where do you live? In the village? And she said, no, she was only visiting. She'd be going home on the bus later. It was Vic who asked her what time the bus left because maybe we could give her a lift home. She told him and Vic said we'd look out for her, because we'd be going along that road ourselves later. Then Vic said to her not to tell anyone about seeing us with the boat because it belonged to his brother and he hadn't asked permission to take it out. He might get mad if he knew we'd borrowed it without asking. And she said, all right, she wouldn't say anything."

"She liked you?" Rudd asked.

Eddy Lisle lowered his eyes.

"Yes," he said. "I think maybe she did."

"So, later, when you pulled up at the bus stop, she accepted a lift?"

"Yes. We took the boat back to Tolquay and Vic looked up the bus time-tables. He didn't want to pick her up in the village in case we were seen, but he saw she'd have to change buses along the route. It was dark, by then. We saw her waiting at the bus stop."

He paused and added violently, "I don't want to talk about it anymore!"

"Then I'll tell you," Rudd replied. "You pulled up and offered her a lift. She accepted, of course. Why shouldn't she? She'd met you already and you seemed a nice, friendly sort of man. Besides, there were two of you. Safety in numbers, or so she thought. You couldn't kill her yourself. You're not the sort. But Vic did. How much, though, did you know of what was going to happen when she got into the passenger seat beside you? Did Vic tell you what he planned to do?"

"I didn't know!" Eddy burst out.

"But you guessed?"

"I swear to God, I didn't! He told me to pull off the road because he thought one of the tyres was flat. I got out to look and when I went back, she was lying with her head against the seat. I could see she was dead. Vic made me help him carry her to the gate and we put her near some bushes. When we got back, we saw her hand-bag lying on the floor. Vic had already asked her if she'd told anybody about meeting us and she said no, there was only her father and he'd been asleep and was a bit bad tempered anyway when he woke up. So we knew we were all right there. But Vic said she might have written down the name of the boat on a bit of paper in her bag. He went through it. I saw the key-ring lying loose in the bottom. Vic said take it, so I took the key off and kept the ring."

"No," said Rudd firmly. "Not Vic, Eddy. Vic wouldn't trouble himself with a cheap little trinket like that. You took it because you fancied it. What was it: sentiment, superstition; the hope it would bring you good luck? A memento of some kind? I think, in a funny sort of way, you rather liked Melanie Thorpe. You were sorry she had to die. But Vic was giving the orders, the same as he always did, and you hadn't got the guts to stand up against him. One thing I'm certain about, you knew damn well there was nothing wrong with the car's tyres when you pulled off the road."

Eddy covered his face and wept with the broken abandon of a child. Rudd watched him for a few seconds without speaking and then signalled the warder to take him away.

After he had gone, he turned wearily to Monk.

"I'll charge him later," he said.

"As accessory before or after?" Monk asked.

Rudd lifted his shoulders.

"I doubt if he'll admit to knowing beforehand that Vic intended killing her. My guess is he did, but he won't admit that, even to himself. Did you notice, he said, 'We put her near some bushes'? She wasn't put, Reg. She was thrown over that gate, like a bundle of old clothes that no-one had any more use for."

He thought of Thorpe, covering up out of the same need to protect his own self-esteem, the fact that he'd drunk himself into a stupor the day Melanie died. Bibby Tucker, too, had the same desperate desire to appear better than he was in his own eyes and in the eyes of others.

"What's the next move?" Monk was asking. "Have Vic Lisle in? Confront him with Eddy's confession?"

"I suppose so," Rudd replied, without much enthusiasm. Having come so far, he felt none of the expected excitement, only a sense of weariness and anticlimax.

Monk looked at him closely and seemed to sense his mood.

"You handled Eddy Lisle very cleverly, I thought," he remarked, hoping the compliment might raise the Inspector's spirits. "I might have guessed myself at the man's vanity; after all, he'd been a good-looking man in his time. But I'd always thought he and Vic were close as brothers. It never crossed my mind they were anything but loyal. I suppose there's no chance Eddy might withdraw his confession at the last minute? He could make out it had been forced out of him under pressure. We know Frank Lisle's got a clever lawyer working for him."

"I don't think so," Rudd replied. "The bitterness between him and Vic goes too deep. Besides, even if he did, we could still get a conviction. There's too much circumstantial evidence against them apart from the key-ring; strong enough this time to convince a jury. No, Eddy knows, it's either him or Vic and he'll shop Vic if only to get his own back. I know the chinks in his armour now. It gives me the advantage."

"You may not find the same weaknesses in Vic," Monk warned him.

"I don't need to," Rudd replied. "I've got enough against him without that. Shall we see him now?"

They interviewed Vic Lisle in McKinley's office. Rudd set it up as a more official and formal occasion this time, with McKinley and Monk seated behind the desk, himself standing.

Vic Lisle, dressed in the prison battle-dress top and trousers, was marched in between two warders and was brought to attention in front of the desk.

Rudd looked him over slowly, taking his time. He recognised him easily from the photographs on the police records. There was no sense of shock as there had been when he first confronted Eddy Lisle. Vic had suffered no physical deterioration as his brother had done. The narrow, dark face seemed not to have changed. He stood stiffly to attention, in the regulation pose, his arms straight at his side, facing forwards, his eyes fixed on a point beyond Rudd's right shoulder at the window behind him.

He made no sign of response as Rudd repeated the words of the official caution.

"Victor Stanley Lisle, you are not obliged to say anything but anything you do say may be taken down in writing and may be used as evidence against you."

A small silence followed and then Rudd took up the examination.

"Mr. Lisle, I am making inquiries into the death of Melanie Ann Thorpe, who was found murdered four years ago. I have reason to believe you were responsible for her death."

Vic Lisle said nothing. After a pause, Rudd continued:

"I believe you met her on the day she was murdered at Mill House Creek, that you arranged to meet her later and that you subsequently picked her up in your car at Hadley Corner and that shortly afterwards you strangled her in a gateway, leaving her body in a field."

As he spoke, he searched Vic Lisle's face, as he had done with Eddy's, for any change of expression. But he found none. The long face remained impassive. The eyes remained fixed on the window.

Beside him, Rudd heard McKinley clear his throat. The silence went on and Rudd found anger begin to rise in him.

"Your brother Eddy has already admitted it was you who murdered her," he added, with more force than he intended.

A small smile touched the corners of Vic Lisle's mouth

and then vanished. What had it indicated? Rudd found it impossible to tell. Amusement? Contempt? A sense of the man's own superiority?

"Have you nothing to say?" Rudd asked.

Vic Lisle's eyes rested momentarily on the Inspector's face and then he withdrew his glance and fixed it once again on the point beyond Rudd's shoulder.

"Take him away," Rudd told the warders and, turning his back, he walked towards the window. Behind him, he heard Vic Lisle being marched off and then Monk and McKinley in low-toned consultation. After a while, the door opened and closed again and someone went out, presumably McKinley, because Monk joined him at the window.

"I've asked McKinley to make arrangements for Vic to be kept in solitary confinement. It's better he and Eddy are kept apart. We'll be transferring them, anyway, to Brixton shortly to face the rest of the charges against them. I suppose you'll want to charge them yourself when they're there."

He sounded subdued, almost apologetic. Rudd nodded briefly and went on staring out of the window.

"I know how you must be feeling . . ." Monk began.

"Do you?" Rudd asked fiercely, turning to face him. "Christ, man, do you know I wanted to smash him as he stood there. I wanted to get him by the throat and choke the life out of him as he did to that kid, Melly. God, Reg, I thought I *understood* criminals."

He put a contemptuous emphasis on the word "understood."

"I knew their weaknesses and their flaws. But I'd always thought of myself as being above them. They were mean, vicious, greedy little men and I was something superior. But Vic Lisle's made me realise something about myself I didn't know before. I'm quite capable of killing, too."

"And that shocks you?" Monk asked.

"Yes, it does," Rudd replied.

"Then don't let it," Monk told him. "I think you've met in Vic Lisle a type of killer who's mercifully rare; the man who murders without pity because he's incapable of feeling it. Thank Christ, I've only seen two other men like him and they both brought me out in a cold sweat. They're real killers; psychopaths who'll take a life with no more feeling than you and I would swat a fly. Let it go. You've got your murderer. The case is closed. Forget it. Forget him. Or if you can't, try to see him as some kind of emotional cripple, a man to be pitied."

"Pitied!" cried Rudd.

"Yes, because he'll never know what it is to feel any kind of human emotion. Even Eddy's better off than he is. But Vic Lisle's totally alone."

Totally alone! A picture rose in Rudd's mind of Thorpe's face, looking up at him from the low door-way of the house-boat and asking, with that look of terrible eagerness, "You'll tell me when you get him?"

"I must go," Rudd said abruptly.

As he drove away, he felt some of the anger die down inside him, although it still smouldered. It was impossible to let it go, as Monk had advised him. He was still too involved in the case.

In Merestead, he parked the car as dusk was falling and walked slowly along the sea-wall towards the house-boat. The marshes stretched away in the fading light, wider than ever it seemed, with a melancholy emptiness of glistening mud that sucked and rustled. Presently, he saw the dark, top-heavy bulk of the house-boat ahead of him, with a faint yellow light shining through the window. The door was shut and a trickle of smoke trailed upwards from the chimney into the darkening sky. The white mongrel, chained to the deck for the night, roused itself and whined.

"Who's there?" came Thorpe's voice. The door opened and the man's head appeared, looking upward suspiciously against the lamp-lit interior of the cabin. "Oh, it's you," he added, without much welcome.

Rudd climbed wearily aboard, Thorpe backing away to let him enter.

"You've got news?" he asked. He seemed to read it in the Inspector's face.

"A man will be charged," Rudd replied.

"When?"

"Later."

"He killed her?"

"Yes. There'll be no doubt about it. The evidence . . ." He passed a hand across his face.

"It's been a long day, Mr. Thorpe. But I wanted to come and give you the satisfaction of knowing . . ."

He used the words without thinking. It was one of those semi-official statements that for him had lost most of its meaning. But Thorpe seemed to find it significant.

"Satisfaction!" he shouted. "There'll be no satisfaction until I see him swinging at the end of a rope. They ought to hang buggers like him. More's the pity they don't anymore."

Looking into the man's face, convulsed with rage, Rudd felt his own anger finally die away, leaving only shame and an overwhelming sense of the futility of it all.

"I'm sorry," he said, but he wasn't sure himself for what he was apologising.

Ducking his head, he scrambled out of the boat and up the bank.

Below him on the deck the dog whined and rattled its chain, but he took no notice of it and set off for the scattered lights of the village, walking purposefully away.

The case is closed, he told himself. Remember that. The case is bloody closed.

ABOUT THE AUTHOR

JUNE THOMSON's previous Detective Rudd novels include
A Question of Identity, Death Cap, The Long Revenge
and *The Habit of Loving*. She lives in the beautiful Essex
countryside outside of London.